No one writes romantic fiction like Barbara Cartland.

Miss Cartland was originally inspired by the best of the romantic novelists she read as a girl —writers such as Elinor Glyn, Ethel M. Dell and E. M. Hull. Convinced that her own wide audience would also delight in her favorite authors, Barbara Cartland has taken their classic tales of romance and specially adapted them for today's readers.

Bantam is proud to publish these novels—personally selected and edited by Miss Cartland—under the imprint

**BARBARA CARTLAND'S
LIBRARY OF LOVE**

Barbara Cartland's Library of Love series

Barbara Cartland's Ancient Wisdom series

Barbara Cartland's Library of Love
The Amateur Gentleman
by Jeffrey Farnol

Condensed by Barbara Cartland

BANTAM BOOKS
TORONTO · NEW YORK · LONDON

THE AMATEUR GENTLEMAN
A Bantam Book / August 1978

ISBN 0–553–11892–7

Published simultaneously in the United States and Canada

Bantam Books are published by Bantam Books, Inc. Its trade-
mark, consisting of the words "Bantam Books" and the por-
trayal of a bantam, is registered in the United States Patent
Office and in other countries. Marca Registrada. Bantam
Books, Inc., 666 Fifth Avenue, New York, New York 10019.

PRINTED IN THE UNITED STATES OF AMERICA

Introduction
by
Barbara Cartland

This is a story of adventure, daring, and love. And who could be more entrancing than the gloriously beautiful, proud, unpredictable heroine?

But I lost my heart irretrievably many years ago to the handsome, brave, honest Barnabas, who thought he had lost the fight for his heart's desire, only to find, in the last round, that he had won!

Chapter
One

John Barty, ex-Champion of England, and Landlord of the Coursing Hound, sat screwed round in his chair with his eyes turned to the door that had closed after the departing Lawyer fully five minutes ago.

His eyes were wide and blank, and his mouth gaped.

"Seven 'undred thou'! No! I can't believe it, Barnabas, my boy."

"Neither can I, Father," said Barnabas, still staring down at the papers which littered the table before him.

"Now, what astonishes me is why my brother Tom should leave all this money to you, Barnabas. You, as he never saw but once, and you then an infant in your blessed mother's arms, Barnabas, a-squaring away wi' your little pink fists as proper as ever I seen inside the Ring or out.

"You was a promising infant. If you'd been

governed by me and Natty Bell you might ha'
done us all proud in the Prize Ring."

"But you see, Father . . ."

"If you'd only followed your nat'ral gifts,
Barnabas, I say you might ha' been Champion of
England today."

"I'm sorry, Father, but as I told you . . ."

"Not as I quarrels wi' your reading and writing, Barnabas, no, and because why?

"Because reading and writing is apt to be
useful now and then, because it were a promise as
I made to your mother. When your mother were
alive, Barnabas, she used to keep all my accounts
for me.

"When she died she made me promise as you
should be taught to read an' cypher—an' taught
I've had you, according—for a promise is a promise, Barnabas—an' there y' are."

"For which I can never be sufficiently grateful, both to her—and to you!" said Barnabas.

He sat with his chin propped upon his hand,
gazing through the open lattice to where the broad
white road wound away betwixt blooming hedges,
growing ever narrower till it vanished over the
brow of a distant hill.

"And now I come to your uncle Tom, an'
speaking of him, Barnabas, my lad—what are ye
going to do wi' all this money?"

Barnabas turned from the window and met
his father's eye.

"Do with it?" he began. "Why, first of
all . . ."

"Because," pursued his father, "we might
buy the White Hart t' other side of Sevenoaks. To

be sure, you're over-young to have any say in the matter—still, after all, the money's yours, Barnabas—what d' ye say to the White Hart?"

"Buy whichever you choose, Father, it will all be one to me! You see, I intend to go away, Sir."

"Eh?" exclaimed his father, staring. "Go away—where to?"

"To London!"

"And what should a slip of a lad of twenty-two want in London? You leave London alone, Barnabas. London indeed! What should you want wi' London?"

"Learn to be a gentleman."

"Barnabas, did you say a gentleman, Barnabas?"

"Yes."

"What—you?" Here John Barty's frown vanished suddenly, and, expanding his great chest, he threw back his head and roared with laughter.

"So you want to be a gentleman—hey?"

"Yes."

"You aren't crazed in your head, are ye, Barnabas?"

"Not that I know of, Father."

"This here fortun' then, it's been an' turned your brain, that's what it is."

Barnabas smiled and shook his head.

"Listen, Father," he said, "it has always been the dream and ambition of my life to better my condition, to strive for a higher place in the world —to be a gentleman.

"This was why I refused to become a pugilist, as you and Natty Bell desired. This was why

I worked and studied—ah! a great deal harder than you ever guessed, though up till today I hardly dared hope my dream would ever be realised—but now . . ."

"Now you want to go to London and be a gentleman—hey?"

"Yes."

"Which all comes along o' your reading o' fool books. Why, Lord! You can no more become a gentleman than I can or the—blunderbuss yonder. And because why? Because a gentleman must be a gentleman born, and his father afore him, and *his* father afore him.

"Yes, Barnabas, you was born the son of a Champion of England, an' that should be enough for most lads. But your head's chock-full of fool's notions an' crazy fancies, an' as your lawful father it's my bound duty to get 'em out again, Barnabas, my lad."

So saying, John Barty proceeded to take off his coat and belcher neckerchief, and rolled his shirt-sleeves over his mighty forearms, motioning Barnabas to do the like.

Thus, without more ado they faced each other, foot to foot, bare-armed, and alert of eye. For a moment they sparred watchfully, then John Barty feinted Barnabas into an opening; in that same moment his fist shot out and Barnabas measured his length on the floor.

"Are ye still minded to go to London?"

"Of course."

"Then we'll go on till you think better of it —or till you knock me down, Barnabas, my lad."

4

"Why then, Father, the sooner I knock you down the better."

And now they fell to it in silence, a grim silence broken only by the quick tread and shuffle of feet and the muffled thud of blows.

Twice Barnabas staggered back to the wall, and there was an ugly smear upon his cheek. Yet as they struck and parried, and feinted, Barnabas, this quick-eyed, swift-footed Barnabas, was smiling also.

Then came a rush of feet, the panting hiss of breath, the shock of vicious blows, and John Barty, the unbeaten ex-champion of all England, threw up his arms, staggered back the length of the room, and went down with a crash.

For a moment Barnabas stood wide-eyed, panting, then ran towards him with hands outstretched, but in that moment the door was flung open, and Natty Bell stood between them.

" 'Tis proud you should be to lie there and know as you have a son as can stop even your rush wi' his left an' down you wi' his right. John, we shall see this lad Champion of England yet."

John frowned and shook his head.

"No," he said, "Barnabas'll never be Champion, Natty Bell—there aren't a fighting man in the Ring today as could stand up to him, but he'll never be Champion because he prefers to go to London an' try to turn himself into a gentleman."

"London!" exclaimed Natty Bell. "A gentleman—our Barnabas—what?"

"Well, you must know, then, his uncle, my scapegrace brother Tom—you'll mind Tom as sailed away in a emigrant ship? Well, Natty Bell, Tom has took an' died an' left a fortune to our lad here."

"A fortune, John! How much?"

"Seven hundred thousand pounds."

Natty Bell opened his mouth, shut it, thrust his hands down into his pockets, and brought out a short clay pipe.

"Yes, a good deal can be done wi' such a sum as that, John."

"But it can't make a silk purse out of a sow's ear, Natty Bell, nor yet a gentleman out o' you or me—or Barnabas here."

"But I believe," said Barnabas, frowning down at the empty hearth, "I'm sure that gentility rests not so much on birth as upon hereditary instinct."

"Instinct!" repeated John Barty. "No, you can't come instinct over human beings, Barnabas, my lad. A gentleman is nat'rally born a gentleman as' his father afore him an' his grandfather afore him, back an' back. . . ."

"And," pursued Natty Bell, "if you were the best-dressed, the handsomest, the strongest, the bravest, the cleverest, the most honourable man in the world—that wouldn't make you a gentleman.

"I tell you, Barnabas, if you went among 'em and tried to be one of 'em, they'd find you out someday an' turn their gentlemanly backs on you."

"Ah," nodded John, "and serve you right,

lad, because if you should try to turn yourself into a gentleman, why, Lord, Barnabas! you'd only be a sort of amitoor after all, lad."

"Then," said Barnabas, rising from his chair and crossing with resolute foot to the door, "then, just as soon as this law business is settled and the money is mine, an Amateur Gentleman I'll be."

* * *

It was upon a certain glorious morning some three weeks later that Barnabas fared forth into the world.

Striding blithely upon his way, he might have been the Spirit of Youth itself, head high, eyes a-dance, his heart light as his step, his gaze ever upon the distance ahead, for he was upon the road at last, and every step carried him nearer the fulfilment of his dream.

At Tonbridge he would take the coach, he thought, or perhaps hire a chaise and ride to London like a gentleman. A gentleman! And here he was whistling away like any plough-boy.

Happily, the road was deserted at this early hour, but Barnabas shook his head at himself reproachfully, and whistled no more—for a time.

But now, having reached the summit of the hill, he paused and turned to look back. Below him lay the old Inn, blinking its many casements in the level rays of the newly risen sun.

But now, all at once, as he gazed down at it from this eminence, it seemed somehow to have shrunk, to have grown more weather-beaten and worn. Truly, never had it looked so small and mean as it did at this moment.

7

'Was the change really in the old Inn, or in himself?' he wondered.

He sighed and, turning, went on down the hill. But now, as he went, his step lagged and his head drooped.

'Was the change in the Inn, or could it be that money can so quickly alter one?' he wondered.

And straightaway the coins in his pocket chinked and jingled "yes, yes!" whereupon Barnabas sighed again and his head drooped lower yet.

Well then, since he was rich, he would buy his father a better Inn—the best in all England. A better Inn! And the Coursing Hound had been his home for as long as he could remember.

Here Barnabas sighed yet again, and his step was heavier than ever as he went on down the hill.

Now in a while Barnabas came to where there was a stile with a path beyond, a narrow path that led up over a hill until it lost itself in a wood, where a stream ran gurgling in the shade of osiers and willows; it was a wood that Barnabas had known from boyhood.

Therefore, setting his hand upon the stile, he vaulted lightly over, with a mind to go through the wood and join the high road farther on.

He strode on up the winding path, whistling as he went, plunged into the green twilight of the wood, and, whistling still, swung suddenly into a broad and grassy glade splashed green and gold with sunlight.

And then he stopped all at once and stood there, silent, dumb, the very breath in check between his lips.

She lay upon her side, full length upon the sward, and her tumbled hair made a glory in the grass, a golden mane. Beneath this silken curtain he saw dark brows that frowned a little, a vivid mouth, and lashes thick and dark that curled upon the pillow of her cheek.

Motionless stood Barnabas, with eyes that wandered from the small, polished riding-boot with its delicately spurred heel, to follow the gracious line that swelled voluptuously from knee to rounded hip, and sank in sweetly to a slender waist, yet rose again to the rounded beauty of her bosom.

So Barnabas stood, and looked, then stole a step nearer, and stopped again.

For the leafy screen was parted suddenly, and Barnabas beheld two boots—Hessian boots, elegant, glossy, and betasseled. Glancing higher, he observed a coat of bottle green, high-collared, close-fitting, and with silver buttons.

A coat that served but to make more apparent the broad chest, powerful shoulders, and lithe waist of its wearer. Indeed a truly marvellous coat; and in that moment, for the first time, he became aware of how clumsy and ill-contrived were his own garments.

As for his boots, blunt of toe, thick-soled, and ponderous, he positively blushed for them.

Here it occurred to him that the wearer of the coat possessed a face, and he looked at it accordingly. It was a handsome face he saw, dark of eye, square-chinned, and full-lipped.

Just now the eyes were lowered, lost in leisurely contemplation of she who lay outstretched;

9

and as his gaze wandered to and fro over her defenceless beauty, a glow dawned in his eyes, and the full lips parted in a slow smile, whereat Barnabas frowned darkly, and his cheeks grew hot.

"Sir!"

Then, very slowly and unwillingly, the gentleman raised his eyes and stared across at him.

"And pray," said he carelessly, "who might you be?"

At his tone Barnabas grew more angry and therefore more polite.

"Sir, that—permit me to say—does not concern you!"

"Not in the least, and so I bid you good-day! You can go, my man; I am acquainted with this lady, and she is quite safe in my care."

"That, Sir, I humbly beg leave to doubt."

"Why, you impudent scoundrel!

"Come, take yourself off!" said the gentleman, frowning. "I'll look after this lady."

"Pardon me, but I think not."

The gentleman stared at Barnabas through suddenly narrowed lids, and laughed softly, and Barnabas thought his laugh worse than his frown.

"Ha! D' you mean to say you—won't go?"

"With all the humility in the world, I do, Sir."

"Why, you cursed, interfering yokel! Must I thrash you?"

Now "yokel" stung, for Barnabas remembered his blunt-toed boots. He smiled with lips suddenly grim, and his politeness grew almost aggressive.

"Thrash me, Sir; indeed I almost venture to fear that you must."

But the gentleman's gaze had wandered to the fallen girl once more, and the glow was back in his roving eyes.

"Pah! If it is her purse you are after—here, take mine, and leave us in peace."

As he spoke he flung his purse towards Barnabas, and took a long step nearer the girl.

But in that same instant Barnabas strode forward also, and, being nearer, he reached her first, and stepping over her it thus befell that they came face to face within a foot of each other.

For a moment they stood like this, staring into each other's eyes, then without a word, swift and sudden, they closed and grappled.

Suddenly the bottle-green coat ripped and tore as its wearer broke free. There was the thud of a blow, and Barnabas staggered back with blood upon his face; but in that moment, as his antagonist rushed, Barnabas laughed, fierce and short, and stepped lightly aside and smote him clean and true under the chin, a little to one side.

The gentleman's fists flew wide, he twisted upon his heels, pitched over upon his face, and lay still.

Smiling still, Barnabas looked down upon him, then grew grave.

"Indeed," said he, "indeed it was a great pity to spoil such a wonderful coat."

So he turned away, and coming to where she, who was the unwitting cause of all this, yet lay, he stopped all at once, for it seemed to him that her posture had altered. Her habit had become

11

more decorous, and yet the lashes, so dark in contrast to her hair, those shadowy lashes yet curled upon her cheek.

Barnabas stooped, raised her in his arms, and bore her away through the wood towards the dim recesses where, hidden in the green shadows, his friend the brook went singing upon its way.

In a while the gentleman stirred, sat up, and, beholding his torn coat, swore viciously; then, chancing upon his purse, he pocketed it.

And so he went upon his way, and by contrast with the glory of the morning his frown seemed the blacker.

*   *   *

Coming to where the bending willows made a leafy bower, Barnabas laid her there. Then, turning, he went down to the brook, and drawing off his neckerchief, began to moisten it in the clear, cool water.

The curling lashes were lifted suddenly, and beneath their shadows two eyes looked out, deep and soft and darkly blue, the eyes of a maid—now frank and ingenuous, now shyly troubled, but brim-full of witchery ever and always.

As she lay she gazed upon him in her turn, as he had first looked upon her, pleased to find his face so young and handsome, to note the breadth of his shoulders, the graceful carriage of his limbs, and his air of virile strength and latent power.

Yet she was doubtful too, because of her sex, because of the loneliness, and because he was a man; thus, she lay, blushing a little, sighing a little, fearing a little, and waiting for him to turn.

True, he had been almost reverent so far, but then the place was so very lonely. And yet . . .

Barnabas turned and came striding up the bank. And how was he to know anything of all this as he stood above her with his dripping neckerchief in his hand?

How was he to know how her heart leapt in her white bosom as he sank upon his knees beside her?

But in that moment she sighed, her white lids fluttered, and sitting up she stared at him as though—for all the world as though she had never beheld him until that very moment.

"What are you going to do?" she demanded, drawing away from the streaming neckerchief. "Who are you? Why am I here, what has happened? Where am I?"

"In Annersley Wood, Madam."

"Ah, yes, I remember. My horse ran away."

"So I brought you here to the brook."

"Why?"

"You were hurt; I found you bleeding and senseless."

"Bleeding!" And on the instant, out came a dainty laced handkerchief.

"There," he said, "though indeed it is very trifling."

"Indeed, Sir, it pains atrociously!" she retorted, and to bear out her words showed him her handkerchief, upon whose snowy whiteness was a tiny vivid stain.

"Then perhaps I'd better bathe it with this!" he said, and held up his dripping neckerchief.

"Nay, Sir," she answered. "I thank you, but
13

keep it for your own wounds; there is a cut upon your cheek."

"A cut!" repeated Barnabas, bethinking him of the gentleman's signet ring.

"Yes, a cut, Sir. Pray, did your horse run away also?"

"No, it was not my horse."

"Why then, pray, how did it happen?"

"Happen, Madam? Why, I fancy I must have scratched myself," returned Barnabas, beginning to wring out his neckerchief.

"Scratched yourself. Ah, of course!" she said.

She was silent while Barnabas continued to wring the water from his neckerchief.

"Pray, do you often scratch yourself until you bleed? 'Tis surely a most distressing habit."

Now glancing up suddenly, Barnabas saw that her eyes were wonderfully bright, for all her solemn mouth, and suspicion grew upon him: 'Does she know? Did she see?' he wondered.

"Nevertheless, Sir, my thanks are due to you. . . ."

"For what?"

"Why for . . . for . . ."

"For bringing you here?"

"Yes. Believe me, I am more than grateful for . . . for . . ."

"For what, Madam?" he enquired again, looking at her now.

"For . . . your . . . kindness, Sir."

"Pray, how have I been kind? You refused my neckerchief."

"Sir," she said, with her dimpled chin a little higher than usual, "it is a great pity you troubled yourself about me, and spoilt your neckerchief with water."

"I thought you were hurt, you see. . . ."

"Oh, Sir, I grieve to disappoint you," she said, and rose.

Indeed, she gained her feet with admirable grace and dignity, notwithstanding her recent fall and the hampering folds of her habit; and now Barnabas saw that she was taller than he had thought.

"Disappoint me!" repeated Barnabas, rising also. "The words are unjust."

For a moment she stood, her head thrown back, her eyes averted disdainfully, and it was now that Barnabas first noticed the dimple in her chin.

He was observing it very exactly when he became aware that her haughtiness was gone again and that her eyes were looking up at him, half-laughing, half-shy, and of course wholly bewitching.

"Yes, I know they were," she admitted, "but oh, won't you please believe that a woman can fall off her horse without being hurt, and that it won't bleed much."

Now as she spoke a distant clock began to strike and she to count the strokes, soft and mellow with distance.

"Nine!" she exclaimed with an air of tragedy. "Now I shall be late for breakfast, and I'm ravenous . . . and, gracious heavens!"

"What now, Madam?"

"My hair! It's all come down . . . look at it!"

"I've been doing so every since I met you," Barnabas confessed.

"Oh, have you! Then why didn't you tell me of it ... and I've lost nearly all my hair-pins ... and ...oh dear! what will they think?"

"That it is the most beautiful hair in all the world, of course," said Barnabas.

She was already busy twisting it into a shining rope, but here she paused to look up at him from under this bright nimbus, and with two hair-pins in her mouth.

"Oh, do you think so?"

"Yes," said Barnabas, steady-eyed.

Immediately, down came the curling lashes again, while with dexterous white fingers she began to transform the rope into a coronet.

"I'm afraid it won't hold up," she said, giving her head a tentative shake, "though fortunately I haven't far to go."

"How far?"

"To Annersley House, Sir."

"Yes, that is very near; the glade yonder leads into the park."

"Do you know Annersley then, Sir?"

Barnabas hesitated and, having gone over the question in his mind, shook his head.

"I know of it."

"Do you know Sir George Annersley?"

"We are not exactly acquainted, Madam."

Yesterday he would have scorned the subterfuge; but today there was money in his purse, London awaited him with expectant arms, and the very air was fraught with a magic whereby the impossible might become reality.

Was not she herself, as she stood before him lithe and vigorous in all the perfection of her warm young womanhood—was she not the very embodiment of those dreams that had haunted him sleeping and waking? Verily.

"Are you going far, Sir?"

"To London."

"Have you many friends there?"

"None—as yet, Madam."

After this they walked on in silence, she with her eyes on the look-out for obstacles, he lost to all but the beauty of the young body before him, the proud carriage of the head, the sway of the hips, the firm poise of the small and slender feet.

All this he saw and admired, yet his face bore nothing of the look that had distorted the features of the gentleman in the bottle-green coat, though to be sure our Barnabas was but an amateur at best.

So at last she reached the fateful glade beyond which was a noble house set upon a gentle hill. Here my lady paused; she looked up the glade and down the glade and finally at him.

Her eyes were the eyes of a maid, shy, mischievous, demure, challenging.

"Sir," she said, shyly, demurely, but with eyes still challenging, "Sir, I have to thank you. I do thank you . . . more than these poor lips can tell. If there is anything I could . . . do . . . to prove my gratitude, you . . . have but to . . . name it."

"Do? Do—indeed—I—no," stammered Barnabas.

The challenging eyes were hidden now, but the lips curved, wonderfully tempting and full of allurement.

Barnabas clenched his fists hard.

17

"I see, Sir, your cheek has stopped bleeding; 'tis almost well. I think there are others whose hurts will not heal quite so soon, and between you and me, Sir, I'm glad . . . glad! Good-bye! and may you find as many friends in London as you deserve."

So saying, she turned and went on down the glade.

And in a little while Barnabas sighed, and, turning also, strode on towards London.

Now when she had gone but a very short way she stopped to watch him as he swung along, strong, graceful, but with never a look behind.

'Who is he?' she wondered. 'What is he? From his clothes he might be anything between a game-keeper and a farmer.'

He had never told his name, nor—what was a great deal worse—had he asked for hers. Here my lady frowned, for such indifference was wholly new in her experience.

But on went Barnabas, all unconscious, with never a look behind.

Then all at once the frown vanished and was replaced with a sudden smile, and she instinctively shrank closer into cover, for Barnabas had stopped.

'Oh, indeed, Sir! So you've actually thought better of it, have you?' she thought.

Here Barnabas turned.

'Really, Sir, you will even trouble to come all the way back, will you, just to learn my name? But, dear Sir, you're too late . . . oh yes, indeed your are! "For he who will not when he may,

18

when he will he shall have nay." Good-morning,
Master Shill-I-shall-I.'

With that thought she turned, then hastily
drew a certain lace handkerchief from her bosom,
and set it very clearly among the thorns of a
bramble, and so sped away among the leaves.

"Now, by the Lord!" said Barnabas to himself, stopping all at once. "Forgetful fool that I
am! I never bowed to her!"

He turned sharply about, and came striding
back again, and thus it befell that he presently
cspicd the lace handkerchief fluttering from the
bramble, and having extricated the delicate lace
from the thorns he began to look about for the
owner.

But search how he might, his efforts proved
unavailing—Annersley Wood was empty save for
himself.

Barnabas sighed again, thrust the handkerchief into his pocket, and once more set off upon
his way.

"I wonder who she was—I might have asked
her name, but, fool that I am, I even forgot that!"
he said to himself.

Here Barnabas sighed again.

"And yet, had she told me her name, I
should have been compclled to announce mine,
and Barnabas Barty—hum! Somehow there is no
suggestion about it of broad acres or knightly an-
cestors. No, Barty will never do. Mortimer
sounds better, or Mandeville.

"Then there's Neville, and Desborough, and
Ravenswood—all very good names, and yet none
19

of them seems quite suitable. Still, I must have a name that is beyond all question!"

Barnabas walked on, more thoughtful than ever. All at once he stopped, and clapped hand to thigh.

"My mother's name, of course—Beverley. Yes, it is an excellent name, and since it was hers, I have more right to it than to any other. So Beverley it shall be—Barnabas Beverley—good!"

Here Barnabas stopped and very gravely lifted his hat to his shadow.

"Mr. Beverley," said he, "I salute you, your very humble, obedient servant. Mr. Beverley, Sir, God keep you!"

Hereupon he put on his hat again and fell into his swinging stride.

He had not gone far when he came upon another traveller, and, entering into conversation with him, Barnabas declared his intention of going to London to become a gentleman in the World of Fashion.

"In the World of Fashion, Sir, there are gentlemen left!" his companion replied. "This is the age of your swaggering, prize-fighting Corinthians. London swarms with 'em, Brighton's rank with 'em, they pervade even these solitudes!

"I saw one of 'em only half-an-hour ago, limping out of a wood yonder. Ah, a polished, smiling rascal—a dangerous rogue. One of your conscienceless young reprobates equally ready to win your money, ruin your sister, or shoot you dead, as the case may be, and all in the approved way of gallantry, Sir.

"And being all this, and consequently high

in Royal favour, he has become a very lion in the World of Fashion. Should you succeed, young Sir, you must model yourself upon him as nearly as may be."

"And he was limping, you say?" enquired Barnabas thoughtfully.

"And serve him right, Sir—egad! I say damme! He should limp in irons to Botany Bay and stay there, if I had my way."

"Did you happen to notice the colour of his coat?" enquired Barnabas again.

"Aye, 'twas green, Sir. But what of it—have you seen him?"

"I think I have, Sir," said Barnabas, "if 'twas a green coat he wore. Pray, Sir, what might his name be?"

"His name, Sir, is Carnaby—Sir Mortimer Carnaby."

"Sir Mortimer Carnaby!" said Barnabas, nodding his head.

"Sir, since it is your ambition to cut a figure in the World of Fashion, your best course is to cultivate him, frequent his society as much as possible, act upon his counsel, and in six months or less I don't doubt you'll be as polished a young blackguard as any of 'em. Good-morning, Sir."

He turned off the road, nodding to Barnabas, who stood for a moment in thought before going on his way.

Chapter
Two

Before him was a church. It stood well back from the road which wound away down the hill to the scattered cottages in the valley below.

A low stone wall was set about it, and in the wall was a gate with a weather-beaten porch, and beside the gate were the stocks, and in the stocks, with his hands in his pockets and his back against the wall, sat a young gentleman.

A lonely figure whose boots, bright and polished, were thrust helplessly enough through the leg-holes of the stocks.

Now observing the elegance of his clothes, and the modish languor of his lounging figure, Barnabas at once recognised him as a gentleman par excellence, and immediately the memory of his own country-made clothes and clumsy boots arose and smote him.

The solitary prisoner seemed in no wit cast down by his awkward and most undignified position; indeed, as Barnabas drew nearer he could hear the prisoner whistling softly to himself.

At the sound of his approach, however, the prisoner glared up from under the brim of his buckled hat and observed him with a pair of the merriest blue eyes in the world.

The face, beneath the devil-may-care rakishness of the buckled hat, was pale and handsome, and, despite their studied air of gentlemanly weariness, the eyes were singularly quick and young, and wholly ingenuous.

Now, as the two men gazed at each other, eye to eye—the merry blue and the steadfast grey —suddenly, unaffectedly, as though drawn by instinct, their hands reached out and met in a warm and firm clasp.

In that instant the one forgot his modish languor, and the other his country clothes and blunt-toed boots, for the Spirit of Youth stood between them and smile answered smile.

"From your direction I guess that you are bound for London, Sir; pray, are you in a hurry to get there?"

"Not particularly."

"Then there you have the advantage of me, for I am, Sir. But here I sit, a martyr for conscience' sake. Now, Sir, if you are in no great hurry, and have a mind to travel in company with a martyr, just as soon as I am free of these bilboes, we'll take the road together. What d' ye say?"

"With pleasure!"

"Why then, Sir, pray, sit down. I blush to offer you the stocks, but the grass is devilishly

24

dewy and damp, and there's deuce a chair to be had—which is only natural, of course; but pray, sit somewhere until my servant produces the key and lets me out."

"And pray," enquired Barnabas, "may I ask what brings you to sit in this place of thought?"

"Well, Sir," pursued His Lordship, "the long and short of it is—my honoured father vows that unless I give up horse-racing and spend less time and money in London, he will clap me into the stocks."

" 'Then, Sir,' says I, smiling and unruffled, 'pray, clap me in as soon as you will;' and he being, as I told you, a man of his word—well, here I am."

"Where I find you enduring your situation with remarkable fortitude," said Barnabas.

"Though I'll admit, 'twixt you and me, Sir, the position cramps one's legs most damnably."

"Pray," said Barnabas suddenly, "do you chance to be acquainted with a Sir Mortimer Carnaby?"

"Acquainted? Oh, Gad, Sir, everyone who *is* anyone is acquainted with Sir Mortimer Carnaby! He is the most admired Buck in London, Sir. The most dashing, the most sought after, a boon companion of Royalty itself."

"Do you mean that he is a personal friend of the Prince?"

"One of the favored few," said the gentleman, nodding.

At that moment his servant arrived, bearing in his pocket a heavy iron key, stolen, it seemed, from under the very nose of the irate parent.

The young man got up, stretched his legs, smiled at Barnabas, and, shaking the hand of his servant, gestured towards the road.

"Sir, shall we be on our way?"

Barnabas agreed readily, and the two of them walked away together down the hill.

"Sir," said the gentleman, after they had gone some way in silence, "you are thoughtful not to say devilish grace!"

"And you," retorted Barnabas, "have sighed —three times."

"No, did I though? Why then, to be candid, I detest saying 'good-bye'! But deuce take me, if we are to become friends, which I sincerely hope, we ought at least to know each other's name.

"Mine, Sir, is Devenham, Viscount Horatio Devenham. I was named Horatio, after Lord Nelson; consequently my friends generally call me Tom, Dick, or Harry, for with all due respect to His Lordship, Horatio is a very devil of a name, now isn't it? Pray, what's yours?"

"Barnabas—Beverley. At your service."

"Barnabas—hum! Yours isn't much better. No, I'll call you Bev, on condition that you make mine Dick; what d' ye say, my dear Bev?"

"Agreed, Dick," answered Barnabas, smiling.

Whereupon they stopped, and, having very solemnly shaken hands, went on again, merrier than ever.

"Now what," the Viscount enquired suddenly, "what do you think of marriage, my dear Bev?"

26

"Marriage?" repeated Barnabas, staring.

"Marriage!" His Lordship nodded, airily. "Matrimony, Bev—wedlock, my dear fellow."

"I—indeed, I have never had occasion to think of it."

"Fortunate fellow!" his companion said, and sighed.

"Until this morning!" added Barnabas, as his fingers encountered a small, soft, lacy bundle in his pocket.

"Unfortunate fellow!" The Viscount sighed, shaking his head. "So you are haunted by the grim spectre, are you? Well, that should be an added bond between us. Not that I quarrel with matrimony, mark you, Bev; in the abstract it is a very excellent institution.

"Though—mark me again—when a man begins to think of marriage, it is generally the beginning of the end. Ah, my dear fellow! many a bright and promising career has been blighted, sapped, snapped off, and—er—ruthlessly devoured by the ravenous maw of marriage.

"There was young Egerton who had a natural gift for boxing, and one of the best whips I ever knew—we raced our coaches to Brighton and back for a thousand a side and he beat me by six yards. A splendid all-round sportsman, ruined by matrimony!

"He's buried somewhere in the country and passing his days in the hum-drum pursuit of being husband and father. Oh, it's all very pitiful, and yet," here the Viscount sighed again, "I do not quarrel with the state, for marriage has often

27

proved a—er—'very present help in the time of trouble,' Bev."

"Trouble?"

"Money troubles, my dear Bev, pecuniary unpleasantnesses, debts, and duns, and devilish things of that kind."

"But surely no man—no honourable man— would marry and burden a woman with debts of his own contracting?"

At this, the Viscount looked at Barnabas somewhat askance, and fell to scratching his chin.

"Of course," he continued somewhat hurriedly, "I shall have all the money I need—more than I shall need—someday. Oh, dammit! Let's talk of something else—Carnaby, for instance."

"Yes," Barnabas nodded, "your friend, Carnaby."

"Well then, in the first place, I owe him five thousand pounds. There's another thousand to Jerningham, but he can wait; then there's six hundred to my tailor, deuce take him!"

"Six hundred!" exclaimed Barnabas, aghast.

"Then, let's see there's another three hundred and fifty to the coach-builders. How much does that make, Bev?"

"Six thousand nine hundred and fifty pounds!"

"So much? Deuce take it! And that's not all, you know."

"No?"

"No, Bev; I dare say I could make you up another three or four hundred or so if I were to rake about a bit, but six thousand is enough to go on with, thank you!"

"Six thousand pounds is a deal of money to owe!" said Barnabas.

"Oh, it might be worse! As it is, Bev, the case lies thus: unless I win the race, some three weeks from now—I've backed myself heavily, you'll understand—unless I win, I am between the deep sea of matrimony and the devil of old Jasper Gaunt."

"And who is Jasper Gaunt?"

"Oh, delicious innocence! Ah, Bev, it's evident you are new to London. Ask it but in a whisper, at Almack's or White's or Brooks's, and they'll tell you, one and all, that Jasper Gaunt is the harshest, most merciless blood-sucker that ever battered and grew rich on the poverty and suffering of his fellow men, and—oh, here we are!"

Saying which, His Lordship abruptly turned down a narrow side-lane, where, screened behind trees, was a Hedge-Tavern with a horse-trough before the door, and a sign that read: THE SPOTTED COW.

The Viscount led Barnabas across the yard to a certain wing or off-shoot of the Inn, where beneath a deep, shadowy gable was a door.

Yet here he must needs pause a moment to glance down at himself to settle a ruffle and adjust his hat before lifting the latch; then he ushered Barnabas into a kitchen.

Ay, but such a kitchen! Surely wood was never whiter nor pewter more gleaming than in this kitchen; surely no flagstones ever glowed a warmer red.

Surely oak panelling never shone with a mel-

29

lower lustre; surely no viands could look more delicious than the great joint upon the polished side-board, flanked by the crisp loaf and the yellow cheese.

And yet—and yet!—sweeter, whiter, warmer, purer, and far more delicious than anything in this kitchen was she who had started up to her feet so suddenly, and now stood with blushing cheeks, gazing shy-eyed upon the young Viscount.

She was all dainty grace from the ribbons in her mob-cap to the slender, buckled shoes peeping out beneath her print gown; and Barnabas, standing between them, saw her flush reflected as it were for a moment in the Viscount's usually pale cheeks.

"My Lord!" she said, and stopped.

"Why, Clemency, you—you—are handsomer than ever!" stammered the Viscount.

"Oh, My Lord!" she exclaimed.

As she turned away Barnabas thought there were tears in her eyes.

"Did we startle you, Clemency? Er—this is a friend of mine—Mr. Beverley—Mistress Clemency Dare. And oh, Clemency, I've had no breakfast!"

But seeing that she yet stood with head averted, the Viscount with a freedom born of long acquaintance, yet with a courtly deference also, took the hand that hung so listlessly, and looked down into the flushed beauty of her face, and as he looked beheld a great tear that crept down her cheek.

"Why, Clemency!" he exclaimed, his raillery gone, his voice suddenly tender. "Clemency—you're crying! My dear, what is it?"

Now beholding her confusion, Barnabas turned away and walked to the other end of the kitchen, and there it chanced that he espied two objects that lay beneath the table, and stooping, forthwith, he picked them up.

They were small and insignificant enough in themselves—being a crumpled scrap of paper and a handsome, embossed coat-button; yet as Barnabas gazed upon this last, he smiled grimly, and, so smiling, slipped the objects into his pocket.

"Come now, Clemency," persisted the Viscount gently, "what is wrong? See how red your eyes are, they quite spoil your beauty. . . ."

"Beauty! Oh, My Lord—even you!"

"What? What have I said? You are beautiful, you know, Clem, and . . ."

"Beauty!" she cried again, and turned upon him with clenched hands, and dark eyes aflame. "I hate it, oh, I hate it!"

With the words she stamped her foot passionately, and turning, sped away, banging the door shut behind her.

"Now, upon my soul!" said the Viscount, taking off his hat and ruffling up his auburn locks. "Of all the amazing contradictory creatures in the world, Bev! I've known Clemency—hum—a goodish time, my dear fellow, but I never saw her like this before. I wonder what the deuce . . ."

But at this juncture a door at the farther end

31

of the kitchen opened, and the Landlord entered.

"Jack," said the Viscount, "what's amiss with Clemency?"

"Clemency? Why, why, where be that niece o' mine?"

"She's run away, Jack. I found her in tears, and I had scarce said a dozen words to her when —hey presto! she's off and away."

"Tears is it, My Lord? And 'er sighed too, I reckon. Eh, My Lord?"

"Why, yes, she may have sighed, but . . ."

"Then it be nought but a touch o' love, My Lord."

"Love!" exclaimed the Viscount, frowning. "Now who the devil should she be in love with?"

"That, My Lord, I can't say, not having yet observed. But now, by your leave, I'll pass the word for breakfast."

As they ate, Barnabas and the Viscount resumed their conversation.

"Now, regarding Mistress Clemency, my dear Bev, what do you think of her?"

"That she is a remarkably handsome girl!"

"Hum! D' you think so?"

"Any man would."

"Yes, I suppose they would."

"Your friend Carnaby undoubtedly does."

"Carnaby! Why, what the devil put him into your head? Carnaby's never seen her."

"There you are quite wrong. He was here this morning."

"Carnaby? Here? Impossible! What under heaven should make you think so?"

"This," said Barnabas, and held out a small, crumbled piece of paper.

The Viscount took it, glanced at it, and his knife clattered onto the floor.

"Sixty thousand pounds, is it sixty or six, Bev? Read it out."

And he thrust the torn paper across to Barnabas, who, taking it up, read as follows:

"... *felicitate you upon your marriage with the lovely heiress, Lady M., failing which I beg most humbly to remind you, my dear Sir Mortimer Carnaby, that the sixty thousand pounds must be paid back on the day agreed upon, namely July 16.*

Your humble, obedient Servant,
Jasper Gaunt."

"Jasper Gaunt!" exclaimed the Viscount. "Sixty thousand pounds. Poor Carnaby! Sixty thousand pounds payable on July sixteenth! Now, the fifteenth, my dear Bev, is the day of the race, and if he should lose, it looks very much as though Carnaby would be ruined, Bev."

"Unless he marries 'the lovely heiress'!" added Barnabas.

"Hum!" said the Viscount, frowning. "I wish I'd never seen this cursed paper, Bev!" And as he spoke he crumpled it up and threw it into the great fireplace. "Where in the name of mischief did you get it?"

"It was in the corner yonder. I also found this." He laid the embossed coat-button on the table. "It was wrenched off, you will notice."

"Yes, torn off! Do you think . . ."

"I think," said Barnabas, putting the button back into his pocket, "that Mistress Clemency's tears are accounted for. . . ."

"By God, Beverley," said the Viscount, an ugly light in his eyes, "if I thought that. . . !"

The hand upon the table became a fist.

"I think that Mistress Clemency is a match for any man—or brute."

But in that moment came a diversion, for Barnabas drew his hand from his pocket, and as he did so, something white fluttered to the floor beside the Viscount's chair.

Both men saw it and both stooped to recover it, but the Viscount, being nearer, picked it up.

He glanced at it, looked at Barnabas with a knowing smile, glanced at it again, and was arrested by certain initials embroidered in one corner; then he stooped his head suddenly, inhaling —its subtle perfume, and so handed it back to Barnabas.

Barnabas took it with a word of thanks and thrust it into an inner pocket, while the Viscount stared at him under his drawn brows.

"Pray," said the Viscount after a while, "pray, are you acquainted with the Lady Cleone Meredith?"

"No."

"Have you ever met the Lady Cleone Meredith?"

"Never."

"Sir, you are a most consummate liar!"

"My Lord, give me leave to remark that he who says so, lies himself most foully."

"Mr. Beverley," said the Viscount, regarding him calm-eyed across the table, "there is a place I know of nearby, a very excellent place, being hidden by trees, a smooth, grassy place—shall we go?"

"Whenever you will, My Lord," said Barnabas, rising.

Forthwith, having bowed to each other and put on their hats, they stepped out into the yard, and so walked until they came to where the grass was very smooth and level.

They faced each other with clenched fists and proceeded to fight.

After a while, Barnabas spoke, dabbing at his bloody mouth.

"Sir," said he, "I trust you are not incommoded at all?"

The Viscount, coming slowly to his elbow and gazing round about him with an expression of some wonder, answered, albeit also pantingly and short of breath:

"On the contrary, Sir, I am vastly enjoying myself. I shall give myself the pleasure of continuing—just as soon as the ground subsides a little."

Therefore Barnabas, still dabbing at his mouth, stepped forward, being minded to aid him to his feet, but before he could do so a voice arrested him.

"Stop!" said the voice.

Now glancing round, Barnabas beheld a man, a small man, slender, whose clothes, old and worn, seemed only to accentuate the dignity and high nobility of his face.

Bare-headed, he advanced towards them, and his hair glistened silvery white in the sunshine, though his brows were dark, like the glowing eyes below.

"And pray, Sir," enquired the Viscount, sitting cross-legged upon the green, "who might you be?"

"I am an Apostle of Peace, young Sir," answered the stranger, "a teacher of forgiveness, though, doubtless, an unworthy one. Now let me see you two clasp hands."

"But, Sir, I went so far as to give this gentleman the lie!" said the Viscount.

"Which I went so far as to—return," said Barnabas.

"But surely the matter can be explained?" enquired the stranger.

Now as they looked upon each other, suddenly, despite his split lip, Barnabas smiled, and in that same moment the Viscount held out his hand.

"My dear Bev, I'm free to confess that I like you better and better—but . . ."

"But?"

"As regards the handkerchief now . . . ?"

"I found it—on a bramble bush—in a wood."

"In a wood!"

"In Annersley Wood. I found a lady there also."

"A lady—oh, egad!"

"A very beautiful woman with wonderful yellow hair!"

36

"The Lady Cleone Meredith! But in a wood."

"She had fallen from her horse."

"How? When? Was she hurt?"

"How, I cannot tell you, but it happened about two hours ago, and her hurt was trifling."

"And you—found her?"

"I also saw her safely out of the wood."

"And did you not know her name?"

"I quite—forgot to ask it, and I never saw her until this morning."

"Why then, my dear Bev," said the Viscount, his brow clearing, "let us go back to breakfast, all three of us."

But now, turning about, they perceived that the stranger had gone; yet, coming to the bridge, they presently espied him sitting beside the stream.

"Sir," said Barnabas, "our thanks are due to you. . . ."

"And you must come back to the Inn with us," added the Viscount; "the ham surpasses description."

"I would like to know what you meant by the 'blood of atonement'," said Barnabas the persistent.

"Sirs," said the stranger. "I once had a daughter, and I loved her dearly, but my name was dearer yet. I was proud of her beauty, but prouder of my ancient name, for I was a selfish man.

"We lived in the country, a place remote and quiet. And so, at last, because she was young and high-spirited, she ran away from my lonely house with one who was a villain.

"I grieved for her, young Sirs, I grieved much because I was lonely, but I grieved more for my honourable name, which she had besmirched.

"One evening she came back to me through the twilight, and flung herself upon her knees before me, and besought my forgiveness with sobs and bitter, bitter tears. Ah, young Sirs! I can hear her weeping yet. The sound of it is always in my ears.

"But being as I say a selfish man, and remembering only my proud and honourable name, I, her father, spurned her from me with reproaches and vile words, such burning, searing words as no daughter should hear her father utter.

"And so, weeping still, she turned away wearily, hopelessly, and I stood to watch her bowed figure till she had crept away into the evening and was gone.

"Thus, Sirs, I drove her from me, I who should have comforted and cherished her; I drove her out into the night with hateful words and bitter curses. Oh, was ever there a sin like mine?

"Therefore I walk these highways, preaching always forgiveness and forgetfulness of self, and so needs must I walk until my days be done, or until—I find her again."

The stranger rose suddenly and so stood with bent head and very still; only his hands gripped and wrung each other. Yet, when he looked up, his brow was serene and a smile was on his lips.

"But you, Sirs, you are friends again, and

that is good, for friendship is a blessed thing. And you have youth and strength, and all things are possible to you, therefore. But oh, beware of self; taking the warning of a selfish man—forget self, and so may you achieve great things."

So saying, the stranger turned from them and went upon his way, limping a little, with his hair gleaming silvery in the sunshine as he went.

"A very remarkable man!" said the Viscount. "And I beg you to remember he said that you and I were ordained to be friends, and by Gad, I think he spoke the truth, Bev!"

"I feel sure of it, Viscount," Barnabas said, and nodded.

"Furthermore, Bev, if you are again 'Bev' to me, I must again be 'Dick' to you henceforth—amen and so forth!"

"Agreed, Dick!"

"Then, my dear Bev?" said the Viscount impulsively.

"Yes, my dear Dick?"

"Suppose we shake hands on it?"

"Willingly, Dick; yet first I think it but honourable to tell you that I love the Lady Cleone Meredith."

"Eh—what?" exclaimed the Viscount, falling back a step. "You love her? The devil you do! Since when?"

"Since this morning."

"Love her! But you've seen her but once in your life."

"True," said Barnabas, "but then, I mean to see her many times henceforth."

"Ah! The deuce you do!"

"Yes," answered Barnabas. "I shall possibly marry her—someday."

"Marry—Cleone Meredith?" said the Viscount at last.

"Marry her—yes," said Barnabas slowly.

"Why then, in the first place let me tell you that she's devilishly high and proud."

" 'Tis so I would have her!"

"And cursedly hard to please."

"So I should judge her."

"And heiress to great wealth."

"No matter for that."

"And full of whims and fancies."

"And therefore womanly."

"My dear Beverley," said the Viscount, smiling, "I tell you, the man who wins Cleone Meredith must be stronger, handsomer, richer, and more accomplished than any 'Buck,' 'Corinthian,' or 'Macaroni' of 'em all. . . ."

"Or more determined!"

"Or more determined, yes." The Viscount nodded.

"Then I shall certainly marry her—someday," said Barnabas.

"Hum!" said the Viscount at last. "So it seems that in finding a friend I have also found myself another rival."

"I greatly fear so," said Barnabas, and they walked on together.

But after they had gone some distance in moody silence, the Viscount spoke.

"Beverley," said he, "forewarned is forearmed!"

"Yes," answered Barnabas, "that is why I told you."

At that moment the Viscount's servant appeared, a small imp of a boy called Milo.

"I believe you've been fighting again—come here!" said the Viscount.

"Fighting, M'Lud. What, me?"

"What's the matter with your face—it's all swollen! There, your cheek!"

"Swellin', M'Lud? I don't feel no swellin'."

"No, no—the other cheek."

"Oh, this, M'Lud. Oh, 'e done it, 'e did; but I weren't fightin'."

"Who did it?"

"S' Mortimer's friend, 'e done it, 'e did."

"Sir Mortimer's friend. But how in the world?"

"Wi' his fist, M'Lud."

"What for?"

"Cos I kicked 'im, I did."

"You—kicked Sir Mortimer Carnaby's friend!" exclaimed the Viscount. "What in heaven's name did you do that for?"

"Cos you told me to, M'Lud, you did. You sez to me, last week, don't fight 'cept you can't 'elp it, you sez. 'But allus pertect the ladies,' you sez. 'An' if 'e's too big to reach wid your fists—why, use your boots,' you sez, an' so I did, M' Lud."

"So you were protecting a lady, were you, imp?"

"Miss Clemency, ma'am, yes, M'Lud. She's been good ter me, Miss Clemency, Ma'am, 'as—so when I seen 'im struggling an' trying to kiss 'er,

I came in an' I kicked 'im, I did, an' then he turned round an' give me this 'ere."

"And what was Sir Mortimer's friend like?"

"A tall, werry sleepy gentleman, wot smiled, M'Lud."

"Ha!" exclaimed the Viscount, starting. "And with a scar upon one cheek?"

"Yes, M'Lud."

His Lordship frowned.

"That would be Chichester," said he, thoughtfully. "Now I wonder what the devil should bring that fellow so far from London."

"I 'eard 'im talkin' 'bout a lady to S' Mortimer!"

"Did they mention her name?"

"The sleepy one, 'e did, M'Lud. Jist as S' Mortimer climbed into the chaise—'Here's wishing you luck wiv the lovely Meredith,' that's what 'e sez."

"Meredith!" exclaimed the Viscount.

"Meredith, M'Lud, 'the lovely Meredith,' 'e sez, an' then as he stood watching the chaise drive away, 'May the best man win,' sez 'e to himself. 'An' that's me,' sez 'e."

"Boy," said the Viscount, "have the horses put to—at once."

"Werry good, M'Lud."

Touching his small hat, Milo turned and set off as fast as his small legs would carry him.

"Gad!" exclaimed His Lordship. "This is more than I bargained for. I must be off."

"Indeed!" said Barnabas, who for the last minute or so had been watching a man who was

42

strolling idly up the lane, a tall, languid gentleman in a jaunty hat. "You seem all at once in a mighty hurry to get to London."

"London!" repeated the Viscount, staring blankly. "London? Oh, why yes, to be sure, I was going to London, but—hum—the fact of the matter is, I've changed my mind about it, my dear Bev. I'm going back; I'm going to follow Carnaby."

"Ah!" said Barnabas, still intent upon the man in the lane. "Carnaby again."

"Oh, damn the fellow!" exclaimed the Viscount.

"But—he is your friend."

"Hum!" said the Viscount. "But Carnaby is always—Carnaby, and she . . ."

"Meaning the Lady Cleone," said Barnabas. "She is a woman. . . ."

"'The lovely Meredith'!" Barnabas nodded.

"Exactly! And Carnaby is the devil with women."

"But not this woman," answered Barnabas, frowning a little also.

"My dear fellow, men like Carnaby attract all women. . . ."

"That I cannot believe."

"Have you known many women, Bev?"

"No," answered Barnabas, "but I have met the Lady Cleone. . . ."

"Once!"

"Once!" Barnabas nodded.

"Hum," said the Viscount.

"And therefore," added Barnabas, "I don't

think that we need fear Sir Mortimer as a rival."

"That," the Viscount retorted, shaking his head, "is because you don't know him—either."

Hereupon, having come to the Inn and having settled their score, the Viscount stepped out to the stables, accompanied by the round-faced Landlord, while Barnabas, leaning out from the open casement, stared idly into the lane.

And thus he once more beheld the gentleman in the jaunty hat, who stood lounging in the shade of one of the great trees that grew before the Inn, glancing up and down the lane in the attitude of one who waits.

He was tall and slender, and clad in a tight-fitting blue coat cut in the extreme of the prevailing fashion. Beneath his curly-brimmed hat Barnabas saw a sallow face with lips a little too heavy, nostrils a little too thin, and eyes a little too close together.

At least, so Barnabas thought, but what he noticed more particularly was the fact that one of the buttons of the blue coat had been wrenched away.

Now, as the gentleman lounged there against the tree, he switched languidly at a bluebell that happened to grow within his reach, cut it down, and with gentle, lazy taps beat it slowly into nothingness.

Which done, he drew out his watch, glanced at it, frowned, and was in the act of thrusting it back into his fob when the hedge opposite was parted suddenly and a man came through.

44

A wretched being he looked, dusty, unkempt, unshorn, whose quick, bright eyes gleamed in the thin oval of his pallid face. At sight of this man the gentleman's lassitude vanished, and he stepped quickly forward.

"Well," he demanded, "did you find her?"

"Yes, Sir."

"And a cursed time you've been about it."

"Annersley is farther than I thought, Sir, and . . ."

"Pah! No matter. Give me her answer." The gentleman held out a slim, white hand.

"She had no time to write, Sir," said the man, "but she bade me tell you . . ."

"Damnation!" exclaimed the gentleman, glancing towards the Inn. "Not here, come farther down the lane."

He turned and strode away, with the man at his heels.

"Annersley," said Barnabas, as he watched them go. "Annersley?"

The Viscount, speaking both to him and to the horses, cried:

"Oh, there you are, Bev—stand still, damn you! Jump up, my dear fellow—Gad, they're pulling my arms off!"

"Then you want me to come with you, Dick?"

"My dear Bev, of course I do—stand still, damn you—though we are rivals, we're friends first—so jump up, Bev, and—oh damme, there's no holding 'em—quick, up with you!"

Now as Barnabas stepped forward, afar off

up the lane he chanced to espy a certain jaunty hat, and immediately, acting for once upon impulse, he shook his head.

"Thanks, Dick, but I've decided not to go back."

"What, you won't come then?"

"No."

"Ah, well, we shall meet in London. Enquire for me at White's or Brooks's, anyone will tell you where to find me. Good-bye!"

Then, settling his feet more firmly, he took a fresh grip upon the reins, and glanced over his shoulder to where Milo sat with folded arms in the rumble.

"All right behind?"

"Right, M'Lud."

"Then give 'em their heads—let 'em go!"

The grooms sprang away, the powerful bays reared, once, twice, and then, with a thunder of hoofs, started away at a gallop until the Viscount and the curricle had been whirled into the distance and vanished in a cloud of dust.

"Lord, but this is a great day for the old Spotted Cow, Sir," said the Landlord, as Barnabas yet stood staring down the road. "We aren't had so many o' the Quality here for years.

"Last night the young Vi'count, this morning, bright and early, Sir Mortimer Carnaby and friend, then the Vi'count again, along o' you, Sir, an' now you an' Sir Mortimer's friend. You don't be no ways acquainted wi' Sir Mortimer's friend, be you, Sir?"

"No. What is his name?"

"Well, Sir Mortimer hailed him as 'Chichester,' I fancy, Sir, though I aren't prepared to swear it, and 'twixt you an' me, Sir, he be one o' your fine gentlemen as I aren't no wise partial to, and he's ordered dinner and supper."

"Has he," said Barnabas. "Then I think I'll do the same."

Sitting alone after supper, Barnabas was finishing a letter to his father when he was arrested by a man's voice speaking in a lazy drawl, just outside the open lattice behind him.

"Now 'pon my soul and honour, Beatrix— so much offended virtue for a stolen kiss—begad! You were prodigal of 'em once. . . ."

"How dare you! Oh, coward that you are!" exclaimed another voice, low and repressed, yet vibrant with bitter scorn. "You know that I found you out—in time, thank God!"

"Beatrix?" said Barnabas to himself.

"In time; ah! And pray, who'd believe it? You ran away from me—but you ran away with me—first! In time! Did your father believe it, that virtuous old miser! Would anyone who saw us together believe it? No, Beatrix, I tell you all the world knows you for my . . ."

"Stop!"

A moment's silence, and then came a soft, gently amused laugh.

"Lord, Beatrix, how handsome you are! Handsomer than ever, begad! I'm doubly fortunate to have found you again. Six years is a long time, but they've only matured you—ripened you. Yes, you're handsomer than ever, upon my life and soul you are!"

But here came the sudden rush of flying

draperies, the sound of swift, light footsteps, and Barnabas was aware of the door behind him being opened, closed, and bolted, and thereafter the repressed sound of a woman's passionate weeping.

Therefore, he rose up from the settle, and, glancing over its high back, beheld Clemency.

Almost in the same moment she saw him, and, starting back to the wall, glanced from Barnabas to the open lattice, and covered her face with her hands.

Not knowing what to do, Barnabas crossed to the window and espied again the languid gentleman, strolling up the lane, with his beaver hat cocked at the same jaunty angle, and swinging his stick as he went.

"You—you heard, then!" said Clemency almost in a whisper.

"Yes," answered Barnabas, without turning: "but, being a great rascal, he probably lied."

"No, it is . . . quite true . . . I did run away with him, but oh! indeed, indeed I left him again before . . . before . . ."

"Yes, yes," said Barnabas, a little hurriedly, aware that her face was still hidden in her hands, though he kept his eyes studiously averted.

Then all at once she was beside him, her hands were upon his arm, pleading, compelling; and thus she forced him to look at her, and, though her cheeks yet burned, her eyes met his frankly and unashamedly.

"Sir," said she, "do you believe that I . . . that I found him out in time . . . that I . . . escaped his vileness? You must believe . . . you shall!" And her slender fingers tightened on his arm. "Oh, tell me . . . tell me you believe!"

"Yes," said Barnabas, looking down into the troubled depths of her eyes; "yes, I do believe."

The compelling hands dropped from his arm, and she stood before him, staring out blindly into the glory of the morning; and Barnabas could not but see how the tears glistened under her lashes; also, he noticed how her brown, shapely hands gripped and wrung each other.

"Sir," said she suddenly, "you are a friend of . . . Viscount Devenham."

"I count myself so fortunate."

"And . . . therefore . . . a gentleman."

"Indeed, it is my earnest wish."

"Then you will promise me that, should you ever hear anything spoken to the dishonour of Beatrix Darville, you will deny it."

"Yes," said Barnabas, smiling a little grimly, "though I think I should do—more than that."

Now when he said this, Clemency looked up at him suddenly, and in her eyes there was a glow no tears could quench. Her lips quivered but no words came, and then, all at once, she caught his hand, kissed it, and so was gone, swift and light, and shy as any bird.

Barnabas walked out into the lane and remained staring thoughtfully toward that spot, where he and the Viscount had talked with the Apostle of Peace. And with his gaze bent thitherwards he uttered a name, and the name was:

"Beatrix."

*   *   *

Barnabas walked on along the lane, chin on breast, plunged in a profound reverie, and following a haphazard course, so much so that, chancing presently to look about him, he found that the lane had narrowed into a rough cart-track that wound away between high banks gay with wild-flowers and crowned with hedges, a pleasant, shady spot, indeed, as any thoughtful man could wish for.

Now as he walked, he noticed a dry ditch—a grassy and most inviting ditch; therefore Barnabas sat him down therein, leaning his back against the bank.

"Beatrix," said he again.

As he did so, the hedge almost opposite was burst asunder and a man came slipping down the bank, and regaining his feet stood staring at Barnabas and panting.

A dusty bedraggled wretch he looked, unshaven and unkempt, with quick bright eyes that gleamed in the pale oval of his face.

"What do you want?" Barnabas demanded.

"Everything!" The man panted, with a ghost of a smile on his pallid lips. "But the ditch would do."

"And why the ditch?"

"Because they're after me."

"Who are?"

"Game-keepers!"

"Then, you're a poacher?"

"And a very clumsy one—they had me once —close on me now."

"How many?"

"Two."

50

"Then—hum!—get into the ditch," said Barnabas.

Now the ditch was deep and dry, and the next moment the miserable fugitive was hidden from view by reason of this, and of the grasses and wild-flowers that grew luxuriantly there.

A moment later, a large, red-faced man appeared before Barnabas.

"Did ye see ever a des'prit, poachin' wagabond run down this 'ere lane, Sir?" he enquired.

"No," answered Barnabas.

"But we seen 'im run this way."

"Ah—he must ha' run oop or down this 'ere lane," said his companion, coming up.

"He did neither," said Barnabas.

"Why, then, p'rhaps you be stone blind as well as stone deaf?" suggested the large man.

"Neither one nor the other," answered Barnabas; "and now, since I have answered all your questions, suppose you go and look somewhere else?"

"Look, is it?—look wheer—d' ye mean. . . ?"

"I mean—go."

"Go!" repeated the man, round of eye, "then s'pose you tell us—wheer!"

"Anywhere you like, only—be off!"

The large man glanced at Barnabas again, and strode off, muttering after his companion.

Barnabas became aware that the fugitive had thrust his head out of the ditch, and having glanced swiftly about, was now regarding him out of the corners of his eyes.

"Why do you stare at me?" he demanded suddenly.

51

"I was wondering why you took the trouble and risk of shielding such a thing as I am," answered the fugitive.

"Hum!" said Barnabas. "Upon my soul—I don't know."

"No," said the man, with the ghostly smile upon his lips again, "I thought not."

Now as he looked at the man, Barnabas saw that his cheeks, beneath this stubble, were hollow and pinched, as though by the cruel hands of want and suffering.

Yet in spite of all this and of the grizzled hair at his temples, the face was not old; moreover, there was a merry twinkle in the eye, and a humorous curve of the wide-lipped mouth that appealed to Barnabas.

"And you are a poacher, you say?"

"Yes, Sir, and that is bad, I confess, but what is worse I was, until I took to poaching, an honest man without a shred of character."

"How so?"

"I was discharged—under a cloud that was never dispelled."

"Hum!" said Barnabas. "And what are you by profession?"

"My calling, Sir, was to work for, think for, and shoulder the blame for others—generally fools, Sir. I was a confidential servant, a valet, Sir. And I have worked, thought, and taken the blame for others so very successfully that I must needs take to poaching that I may live."

"But—other men may require valets!"

"True, Sir, and there are plenty of valets to be had—of a sort—but the most accomplished one in the world, if without a character, had better go and hang himself out of the way, and have done with it. And indeed, I have seriously contemplated so doing."

"You rate yourself very highly."

"And I go in rags! Now, to starve, Sir, is unpleasant. Thus, having a foolish though very natural dread of it, I poach rabbits that I may exist. I possess also an inborn horror of rags and dirt.

"Therefore, I exchanged this coat and breeches from a farm-house, the folk being all away in the fields, and though they are awkward, badly made garments, still beggars—and . . ."

"Thieves!" added Barnabas.

"And thieves, Sir, cannot always be choosers, can they?"

"Then you admit you are a thief?"

Here the fugitive glanced at Barnabas with a wry smile.

"Sir, I fear I must. Exchange is no robbery, they say; but my rags were so very ragged, and these garments are at least wearable."

"You have also been a great valet, I understand?"

"And have served many gentlemen in my time."

"Then you probably know London and the Fashionable World?"

"Yes, Sir." said the man, with a sigh.

"Now," pursued Barnabas, "I am given to understand, on the authority of a Person of Quality, that to dress properly is an art."

The fugitive nodded.

"Indeed, Sir, though your Person of Quality

should rather have called it the greatest of all the arts!"

"Why so?"

"Because by dress it is possible to make something out of nothing!"

"Explain yourself."

"Why, there was the case of young Lord Ambleside, a nobleman remarkable for a vague stare, and seldom saying anything but 'What!' or 'Dey-vil take me!' though I'll admit he could curse almost coherently—at times. I found him nothing but a Lord, and very crude material at that, yet in less than six months he was made."

"Made?"

"Made, Sir." The fugitive nodded. "I began him with a cravat, an entirely original creation, which drew the approval of Brummell himself, and, consequently, took London by storm, and I continued him with a waistcoat.

"I finished him with a pair of pantaloons which swept the World of Fashion clean off its legs, and brought him into everlasting favour with the Regent. So My Lord was made, and eventually I married him to an heiress."

"You married him?"

"That is to say, I dictated all his letters, and composed all his verses, which speedily brought the affair to a happy culmination."

"You seem to be a man of many and varied gifts."

"And one—without a character, Sir."

"Nevertheless," said Barnabas, "I think you are the very man I require."

"Sir!" exclaimed the fugitive, staring. "Sir?"

"And therefore," continued Barnabas, "you may consider yourself engaged."

"Engaged, Sir—engaged!" stammered the man. "Me?"

"As my valet." Barnabas nodded.

"But, Sir, I told you—I was—a thief?"

"Yes," said Barnabas, "and therefore I have great hopes of your future honesty."

Now hereupon the man, still staring, rose up to his knees, and with a swift, appealing gesture stretched out his hands towards Barnabas, and his hands were trembling all at once.

"Sir!" said he. "Oh, Sir—d' ye mean it? You don't know, you can't know what such an offer means to me. Sir, you're not jesting with me?"

"No," answered Barnabas, calmly serious of eye, "no, I'm not jesting. And to prove it, here is an advance of wages." And he dropped two guineas into the man's open palm.

The man stared down at the coins in his hand, then rose abruptly to his feet and turned away, and when he spoke again his voice was hoarse.

"Sir," said he, jerkily, "for such trust I would thank you, only words are too poor. But if, as I think it is your desire to enter the World of Fashion, it becomes my duty, as an honest man, to tell you that all your efforts, all your money, would be unavailing, even if you had been introduced by Barrymore, or Hanger, or Vibart, or Brummell himself."

"Ah," said Barnabas, "and why?"

"Because you have made a fatal beginning."

"How?"

"By knocking down the Prince's friend and favourite—Sir Mortimer Carnaby."

For a long moment the two remained silent, each staring at the other, Barnabas still seated in the ditch and the man standing before him, with the coins clutched in his hand.

"Ah!" said Barnabas, at last. "Then you were in the wood?"

"I lay hidden behind a bush, and watched you do it, Sir."

"What were you doing in Annersley Wood?"

"I bore a message, Sir, for the lady."

"Ah!" said Barnabas. "The lady—yes."

"Who lay watching you, also."

"No," said Barnabas, "the lady was unconscious."

"Yet recovered sufficiently to adjust her habit, and to watch you knock him down."

"Hum!" said Barnabas, and was silent awhile. "Have you heard such a name as Chichester?"

"No, Sir."

"And did you deliver the letter?"

"I did, Sir."

"And she—sent back an answer?"

"Yes, Sir."

"The gentleman who sent the letter was tall and slender, I think, with dark hair, and a scar on his cheek?"

"Yes, Sir."

"And when you came back with her answer, he met you down the lane yonder, and I heard you say that the lady had no time to write."

"Yes, Sir. But she promised to meet him at a place called Oakshott's Barn."

"Ah!" said Barnabas. "I think I know it."

"At sunset, Sir!"

"That would be somewhere about half-past seven," mused Barnabas, staring blankly down at his knee.

He was silent so long that his new servant grew fidgety, coughed, and at last spoke.

"Sir," said he, "what are your orders?"

Barnabas started and looked up.

"Orders? Why, first of all, get something to eat, then find yourself a barber, and wait for me at the Spotted Cow."

"Yes, Sir."

The man bowed, turned away, took three or four steps, and came back again.

"Sir," said he, "I have two guineas of yours, and you have never asked my name."

"True," said Barnabas.

"Supposing I go and never come back?"

"Then I shall be two guineas the poorer, and you will have proved yourself a thief, but until you do, you are an honest man so far as I am concerned."

"Sir," said the fugitive, hoarsely, but with a new light in his face, "for that, if I were not your servant—I—should like to—clasp your hand. And, Sir, my name is John Peterby."

"Why then," said Barnabas, smiling all at once, "why then, John Peterby, here it is!"

So, for a moment their hands met, and then John Peterby turned sharply about and strode away down the lane, his step grown light and his head held high.

But, as for Barnabas, he sat there in the ditch, staring at nothing, his heart heavy.

Chapter Three

The sun was getting low as Barnabas parted the brambles and, looking about him, frowned. Before him was Oakshott's Barn.

It was indeed a place of solitude, shut out from the world, closely hidden from observation, a place apt for the meetings of lovers. And therefore, leaning in the shadow of the yawning doorway, Barnabas frowned.

All at once came a rustle of leaves that drew nearer and nearer; yet Barnabas never moved, not even when the bushes were pushed aside and a man stepped into the clearing—a tall, elegant figure, who, having paused to glance sharply about him, strolled on again towards the barn, swinging his tasseled walking-cane, and humming softly to himself as he came.

He was within a yard of Barnabas when he saw him, and stopped dead.

"And who the devil are you?" he enquired at length.

"Sir," said Barnabas, yet leaning in the doorway, "your name I think is Chichester."

"Well?"

"Permit me to return your coat-button!" and Barnabas held out the article in question, but Mr. Chichester never so much as glanced at it.

"What do you want here?" he demanded, soft of voice.

"To warn you that Oakshott's Barn is an unhealthy place—for your sort, Sir."

"To the devil with you and your warning!"

But now Barnabas stepped clear of the doorway, a heavy stick swinging in his hand.

"Mr. Chichester glanced at the heavy stick, at the powerful hand, the broad shoulders, and the resolute face of he who held it, and laughed again, and laughing, bowed.

"Your solicitude for my health—touches me, Sir. I owe you a debt which I shall hope to repay. This place, as you say, is dismal. I wish you good-evening!" Saying which, Mr. Chichester turned away.

But in that same instant Barnabas leapt, and, dropping his stick, caught that slender, jewelled hand, twisted it, and wrenched the weapon from its grasp.

Mr. Chichester stood motionless, white-lipped and silent, but a devil looked out of his eyes.

"Ah!" said Barnabas, glancing down at the pistol he held. "I judged you would not venture into these wilds without something of the sort. The path, you will notice, lies to your left. It is a winding path; I will go with you, therefore, to see that you do not lose your way, and wander back here again."

Without a word Mr. Chichester turned, and coming to the path followed it, walking neither fast nor slow, never once looking to where Barnabas strode behind, and heedless of briar or bramble that dragged at him as he passed.

On they went, until the path lost itself in a grassy lane, until the lane ended in a five-barred gate.

Now, having opened the gate, Mr. Chichester passed through onto the high road, and then for one moment he looked at Barnabas, a long, burning look that took in face, form, and feature, and so, still without uttering a word, he went upon his way.

He walked neither fast nor slow, swinging his tasselled cane as he went, while Barnabas, leaning upon the gate, watched him until his tall, slender figure had merged into the dusk and was gone.

Then Barnabas sighed, and, becoming aware of the pistol in his hand, slipped it into his pocket, for he remembered the devil in the eyes of Mr. Chichester. Then he turned and made his way back to the barn.

* * *

"Dear," said a low, thrilling voice, "have you come at last? Ah! but you are late, and I began to fear that . . ."

The soft voice faltered and broke off with a little gasp, and, as Barnabas stepped out of the shadows, she shrank away, back and back, to the mossy wall of the barn, and leaned there, staring up at him with eyes wide and fearful.

Her hood, closely drawn, served but to enhance the proud beauty of her face, pale under the moon, and her cloak, caught close in one white hand, fell about her ripe loveliness in subtly revealing folds. Now in her other hand she carried a silver-mounted riding-whip.

Because of the wonder of her beauty, Barnabas sighed again, and because of the place where they stood, he frowned; yet when he spoke, his voice was gentle:

"Don't be afraid, Madame, he is gone."

"Gone!" she echoed faintly.

"Yes. We are quite alone; consequently, you have no reason to be afraid."

"Afraid, Sir! I thought—why, 'twas you who startled me."

"Ay," Barnabas nodded, "you expected him!"

"Where is he? When did he go?"

"Some half-hour since."

"Yet he expected me. He knew I should come, why did he go?"

Now hereupon Barnabas lifted a hand to his throat, and loosened his neck-cloth.

"Why then," said he, slowly, "you have—perhaps—met him hereabouts—before tonight?"

"Sir," she retorted, "you haven't answered me. Why did he go so soon?"

"He was forced to, Madame."

"Forced to go . . . without seeing me . . . without one word! Oh, impossible! To hurry away like this, without a word! Oh, why—why did he go?"

"Madame," said Barnabas, "it was because I asked him to."

"But why . . . why?"

"Because, from what little I know of him, I judged it best."

"Sir," she said softly, "Sir . . . what do you mean?"

"I mean that this is such a very lonely place for any woman and such as he."

Now even as Barnabas uttered the words she advanced upon him with upflung head and eyes aflame with sudden passionate scorn.

"Insolent! So it was you . . . you actually dared to interfere?"

"Madame, I did."

Very straight and proud she stood, fierce-eyed and contemptuous of lip.

"And remained to insult me . . . with impunity."

"To take you home again," said Barnabas; "therefore, pray, let us begone."

"With you? No . . . not a step, Sir. When I choose to go, I go alone."

"But tonight," said Barnabas, gentle of voice but resolute of eye, "tonight—I go with you."

"You!" she cried. "A man I have seen but once, a man who may be anything, a . . . a thief, a ploughman, a runaway groom, for aught I know."

She saw Barnabas flinch at this, and the curve of her scornful lips grew more bitter.

"And now I'm going . . . alone. Stand aside and let me pass."

"No, Madame."

"Let me pass, I warn you!"

63

For a minute they fronted each other, eye to eye, very silent and still; then Barnabas smiled and shook his head. And in that very instant, quickly and passionately she raised her whip and struck him across the cheek.

Then as she stood, panting, half-fearful of what she had done, Barnabas reached out and took the whip, and snapped it between his hands.

"And now," said he, tossing aside the broken pieces, "pray, let us go."

"No."

"Why then," sighed Barnabas, "I must carry you again."

Once more she shrank away from him, back and back to the crumbling wall, and leaned there. Then she suddenly covered her face from his eyes, and a great sob burst from her.

Barnabas stopped, and looking at her bowed head and shrinking figure, he knew not what to do. As he stood there, he heard the snapping of a dry twig among the shadows.

Upon the silence stole a rustle of leaves, a whisper that came and went, intermittently, that grew louder and louder, and so was gone again; but in place of this was another sound, a musical jingle like the chime of fairy-bells, very far, and faint, and sweet.

All at once Barnabas knew that his companion's fear of him was gone, swallowed up—forgotten in terror of the unknown.

He heard a slow-drawn, quivering sigh, and then, pale in the dimness, her hand came out to him, crept down his arm, and, finding his hand, hid itself in his warm clasp; and her hand was marvellously cold, and her fingers stirred and trembled in his.

There came again a rustling in the leaves, but louder now, and drawing nearer and nearer, and ever the fairy-chime swelled within the air.

And even as it came, Barnabas felt her closer, until her shoulder touched his, until the fragrance of her breath fanned his cheek, until the warmth of her soft body thrilled through him.

The bushes rustled again, and into the dimness leapt a tall dark figure that sang in a rich sweet voice, and capered among the shadows with a fantastic dancing step, then grew suddenly silent and still.

In that moment the moon shone out again, shone down upon a strange, wild creature, bareheaded and bare of foot.

A very tall man he was, with curling grey hair that hung low upon his shoulders, and upon his coat were countless buttons of all makes and kinds that winked and glittered in the moonlight, and jingled faintly as he moved.

For a moment he stood motionless and staring; then, laying one hand to the gleaming buttons on his bosom, he bowed with an easy, courtly grace.

"Who are you?" demanded Barnabas.

"Billy, Sir, poor Billy."

"And what do you want here?"

"To sing, Sir, for you and the lady, if you will. I sing for high folk and low folk. But tonight I sing for—Them."

"And who are they?"

"The Wise Ones, who, being dead, know all

things, and live on forever. The Wise Ones tell me things. You, now—what do they tell me of you? Hush! You are on your way to London, they tell me—yes—yes, to London town.

"You are rich, and shall feast with Princes, but youth is over-confident and thus shall you sup with beggars. They tell me you came here to-night tasting to save a wanton from herself."

"Fool!" exclaimed Barnabas, turning upon the speaker in swift anger, for my lady's hand had freed itself from his clasp, and she had drawn away from him.

"Fool?" repeated the man, shaking his head. "Nay, Sir, I am only mad, folk tell me. Yet the Wise Ones make me their confidant, they tell me that she—this proud lady—is here to aid an unworthy brother, who sent a rogue instead."

"Brother!" exclaimed Barnabas, with a sudden light in his eyes.

"Who else, Sir?" demanded my lady, very cold and proud again all at once.

"But," stammered Barnabas, "but—I thought . . ."

"Evil of me?"

"No—that is—I—I— Forgive me!"

"Sir, there are some things no woman can forgive. You dared to think . . ."

"Of the rogue who came instead. His name is Chichester."

"Chichester!" she repeated incredulously.

"A tall, slender, dark man, with a scar on his cheek," added Barnabas.

"Do you mean he was here . . . here to meet

me . . . alone? And you . . . you!" she cried, shuddering away from him. "You thought me . . . what . . . he would have made me! You thought I . . . Oh, shame! Ah, don't touch me!"

But Barnabas stooped and caught her hands, and sank upon his knees, and thus, as they knelt together in the moonlight, he drew her so that she must let him see her face.

"My Lady," said he very reverently, "my thought of you is this: that, if such great honour may be mine, I will marry you—tonight."

With her two hands still prisoned in his, and with the tears yet thick upon her lashes, she threw back her head and laughed, with her eyes staring into his.

Barnabas frowned blackly, and dropped her hands, then caught her suddenly in his arms, and held her close.

"By God! I'd kiss you, Cleone, on that scornful, laughing mouth, only—I love you—and this is a solitude. Come away!"

"A solitude," she repeated; "yes, and he sent me here to meet a beast! And now . . . you! You drove away the other brute. Oh! I can't struggle . . . you are too strong . . . and nothing matters now!"

She sighed and closed her eyes.

Then, gazing down upon her rich warm beauty, Barnabas trembled, and loosed her, and sprang to his feet.

"I think we had better go."

But my lady remained crouched upon her knees, gazing up at him under her wet lashes.

"You didn't kiss me!" she said wonderingly.

"You were so helpless!" said Barnabas. "And I honour you because it was your brother."

"Ah, but you doubted me first; you thought I came here to meet that beast!"

"Forgive me," said Barnabas humbly.

"Why should I?"

"Because I love you."

"So many men have told me that," she said, and sighed again.

"But I," said Barnabas, "I am the last, and it is written that 'the last shall be first.' I love you because you are passionate, and pure, and very brave."

"Love!" she exclaimed. "So soon? You have seen me only once!"

"Yes." He nodded. "It is therefore to be expected that I shall worship you also in due season."

Now Barnabas stood leaning upon his stick, a tall, impassive figure. His voice was low, yet it thrilled in her ears, and there was that in his steadfast eyes before which her own wavered and fell; yet, even so, from the shadow of her hood, she must needs question him further.

"Worship me? When?"

"When you are—my wife."

Again she was silent, while one slender hand plucked nervously at the grass.

"Are you so sure of me?" she enquired at last.

"No; only of myself."

"And if I refuse?"

"Then I shall wait."

"Until I wed another?"

"Until you change your mind."

"I think I shall refuse you."

"Indeed, I fear it is very likely."

"Why?"

"Because of my unworthiness. And, therefore, I would not have you kneel while I stand."

"And the grass is very damp." She sighed.

So Barnabas stepped forward with hand outstretched to aid her, but, as he did so, the wandering singer was between them, looking from one to the other with his keen, bright eyes.

"Stay!" said he. "The Wise Ones have told me that she who kneels before you now, coveted for her beauty, besought for her money, shall kneel thus in the time to come. And I, poor Billy, shall stand between you and join your hands thus, and bid you go forth trusting in each other's love and strength. They have told me your name, Barnabas!

"Barnabas—a-ha! that 'minds me—at Barnaby Bright we shall meet again, all three of us, under an orbèd moon, at Barnaby Bright. Farewell, I must begone, farewell till Barnaby Bright. We are to meet again in London town, I think—yes —yes—in London."

And so he bowed, turned, and danced away into the shadows.

And now my lady sighed and rose to her feet, and looking at Barnabas sighed again.

As for Barnabas, he yet stood wondering and looking after the strange creature and pondering his wild words.

Thus my lady, unobserved, viewed him at

her leisure; noted the dark, close-curled hair, the brilliant eyes, the dominating jaw, the sensitive nostrils, the tender curve of the firm, strong mouth.

And she had called him "a ploughman ... a runaway footman." She could see the mark upon his cheek, how red it glowed! 'Did it hurt much?' she wondered.

"Mad, of course—yes, a madman, poor fellow!" said Barnabas thoughtfully.

"And he said your name is Barnabas. So then, your name is . . . Barnabas?"

"Yes. Barnabas Bar—Beverley."

"Beverley?"

"Yes—Beverley. But we must go."

"First, tell me how you learned my name?"

"From the Viscount—Viscount Devenham?"

"Then you know the Viscount?"

"I do; we also know each other as rivals."

"Rivals? For what?"

"Yourself."

"For me? Sir ... Sir ... what did you tell him?"

"My name is Barnabas. And I told him that I should probably marry you, someday."

"You told him . . . that?"

"I did. I thought it but honourable, seeing he is my friend."

"Your friend . . . since when, Sir?"

"Since about ten o'clock this morning."

"Sir ... Sir ... are you not a very precipitate person?"

70

"I begin to think I am. And my name is Barnabas."

"Since ten o'clock this morning! Then you knew me . . . first?"

"By about an hour."

Swiftly she turned away, yet not before he had seen the betraying dimple in her cheek.

And so, side by side, they came to the edge of the clearing.

"Sir," she said very softly. "Sir?"

"My name is Barnabas."

"I fear . . . I . . . does your cheek pain you very much, Mr. Beverley?"

"Thank you, no. And my name is Barnabas."

"I did not mean to . . . to . . ."

"No, no, the fault was mine—I—I frightened you, and indeed the pain is quite gone."

"Quite gone, Sir?"

"Quite gone, and my name is . . ."

"I'm . . . very . . . glad . . . Barnabas."

Four words only, be it noted; yet on the face of Barnabas was a light that was not of the moon, as they entered the dim woodland together.

Their progress through the wood was slow by reason of the undergrowth, yet Barnabas noticed that where the way permitted she hurried on at speed, and moreover that she was very silent and kept her face turned from him.

Therefore he questioned her.

"Are you afraid of these woods?"

"No."

"Of me?"

"No."

"Then, I fear you are angry again."

"I think Barnab ... your name is ... hateful!"

"Strange!" said Barnabas. "I was just thinking how musical it was—as you say it."

"I ... Oh! I thought your cheek was paining you," said she petulantly.

"My cheek? What has that to do with it?"

"Everything, Sir!"

"That," said Barnabas, "that I don't understand."

"Of course you don't!" she retorted.

"Hum!" said Barnabas.

"And now!" she demanded, "pray, how did you know I was to be at Oakshott's Barn tonight?"

"From my valet."

"Your valet?"

"Yes; though, to be sure, he was a poacher, then."

"Sir, pray, be serious!"

"I generally am."

"But why have a poacher for your valet?"

"That he might poach no more, and because I understand that he is the best valet in the world."

Here she glanced up at Barnabas and shook her head.

"I fear I shall never understand you, Mr. Beverley."

"That, time will show. And my name is Barnabas."

"But how did ... this poacher ... know?"

"He was the man who brought you the letter from Mr. Chichester."

"It was written by my brother, Sir."

"He was the man who gave you your brother's letter in Annersley Wood."

"Yes, I remember, in the wood."

"Where I found you lying quite unconscious."

"Where you found me ... yes."

"Lying—quite unconscious!"

"Yes," she answered, beginning to hasten her steps again. "And where you left me without telling me your name ... or ... even asking mine."

"For which I blamed myself—afterwards," said Barnabas.

"Indeed, it was very remiss of you."

"Yes." Barnabas sighed. "I came back to try and find you."

"Really, Sir?" said she, with black brows arched. "Did you indeed, Sir?"

"But I was too late, and I feared I had lost you...."

"Why, that reminds me, I lost my handkerchief."

"Oh!" said Barnabas, staring up at the moon.

"I think I must have dropped it ... in the wood."

"Then, of course, it is gone—you may depend upon that," said Barnabas, shaking his head at the moon.

"It had my monogram embroidered in one corner."

"Indeed," said Barnabas.

"Yes, I was ... hoping ... that you had seen it, perhaps?"

"On a bramble bush," said Barnabas, nodding at the moon.

"Then ... you did find it, Sir?"

"Yes, and I beg to remind you that my name ..."

"Where is it?"

"In my pocket."

"Then why couldn't you say so before?"

"Because I wished to keep it there."

"Please give it to me!"

"Why?"

"Because no man shall have my favours to wear until he has my promise also."

"Then, since I have the one—give me the other."

"Mr. Beverley, you will please return my handkerchief."

Stopping all at once, she held out her hand imperiously.

"Of course," Barnabas sighed, "on the condition ..."

"On no condition, Sir!"

"That you remember my name is Barnabas."

"But I detest your name."

"I am hoping that, by use, it may become a little less objectionable," he said rather ponderously.

"It never can ... never. And I want my handkerchief ... Barnabas."

So Barnabas sighed again, and perforce gave the handkerchief into her keeping. And now it was she who smiled up at the moon; but as for Barnabas, his gaze was bent earthwards.

After they had gone some way in silence he spoke.

"Have you met—Sir Mortimer Carnaby—often?" he enquired.

"Yes," she answered. Then seeing his scowling look, she added, "Very often, oh, very often indeed, Sir!"

"Ha!" said the frowning Barnabas. "And is he one of the many who have—told you their love?"

"And pray, why not, Sir?" she demanded haughtily. "Though indeed it does not at all concern you. And he is at least a gentleman, and a friend of the Prince. . . ."

"And has an excellent eye for horse-flesh—and women," added Barnabas.

She looked at him for a moment, then walked ahead in silence.

But they reached a stile. It was an uncommonly high stile, an awkward stile at any time, more especially at night. Nevertheless, she faced it resolutely, as though Barnabas had ceased to exist.

When, therefore having vaulted over, he would have helped her, she looked over him and past him, and through him, and mounted unaided, confident of herself, proud and supremely disdainful both of the stile and of Barnabas.

And then, because of her pride, or her disdain, or her long cloak, or all three, she slipped, and to save herself must needs catch at Barnabas, and yield herself to his arm; so for a moment she lay in his embrace, felt his tight clasp about her, felt his quick breath upon her cheek. Then he had set her down, and was eying her anxiously.

"Your foot, is it hurt?" he enquired.

"Thank you, no," she answered; and turning with head carried high, she hurried on faster than ever.

"You should have taken my hand," he said, but he spoke to deaf ears.

"You will find the next stile easier, I think," he ventured, but still she hurried on, unheeding.

"You walk very fast!" he said again, but still she deigned him no reply; therefore, he stooped till he might see beneath her hood.

"Dear Lady," he said very gently, "if I offended you a while ago—forgive me—Cleone."

"Oh! I forgive you." She sighed. "It must be nearly ten o'clock."

"I suppose so, and you will naturally be anxious to reach home again."

"Home," she said bitterly; "I have no home. I live in a gaol . . . a prison. Yes, a hateful, hateful prison, and guarded by . . . yes, a tyrant of a guardian!"

Here, having stopped to stamp her foot, she walked on faster than ever.

"Perhaps you don't believe me when I say he is a tyrant?"

"Why, I'm afraid not."

"I'm nineteen!" she said, standing very erect.

"I should have judged you a little older," said Barnabas.

"So I am ... in mind, and ... and experience. Yet here I live, imprisoned in a dreary old house, with nothing to see but trees and roads, and cows and cabbages. I'm watched over and tended from morning till night.

"Oh! There are many kinds of tyrants, and he is one. And so tonight I left him. I ran away to meet ..."

She stopped suddenly, and her head dropped, and Barnabas saw her white hands clench each other.

"Your brother."

"Pray, think of him as kindly as you can," she said, sighing. "You see ... he is only a boy ... my brother."

"So young?"

"Just twenty, but younger than his age, much younger. You see," she went on hastily, "he went to London as a boy ... and ... and he thought Mr. Chichester was his friend, and he lost much money at play, and somehow put himself in Mr. Chichester's power.

"He is my half-brother, really, but I love him so, and I've tried to take care of him ... I was always so much stronger than he ... and ... and so I would have you think of him as generously as you can."

"Yes," said Barnabas, "yes."

"Will you do more? You are going to London. Will you seek him out, will you try to ... save him from himself? Will you promise me to do this? Will you?"

Now seeing the passionate entreaty in her

77

eyes, feeling it in the twitching fingers upon his arm, Barnabas suddenly laid his own above that slender hand, and took it into his warm clasp.

"My Lady," he said solemnly, "I will."

As he spoke he stooped his head low and lower, until she felt his lips warm upon her palm, a long, silent pressure, and yet her hand was not withdrawn.

"Does it seem strange that I should ask so much of you?"

"The most natural thing in the world," said Barnabas.

"But you are a stranger . . . almost!"

"But I love you, Cleone."

After this there fell a silence between them; and having crossed the moonlit meadow, they came to a tall hedge beyond whose shadow the road led away, white under the moon; close by, the ways divided and there stood a weather-beaten finger-post.

Now beneath this hedge they stopped, and neither looked at the other.

"Sir," she said, after a pause, "I would thank you, if I could . . . for all that you have done for me. Words are poor things, I know, but how else may I show my gratitude?"

"You might—kiss me—once, Cleone."

Now here she must needs steal a swift look at him, and thus she saw that he still stared at the ancient finger-post, and that his hands were tightly clenched.

"I only ask," he continued heavily, "for what I might have taken."

"But didn't!" she added, with lips and eyes grown suddenly tender.

"No," Barnabas sighed, "nor shall I ever—until you will it so—because, you see, I love you."

Now as he gazed at the finger-post, even so she gazed at him, and she saw again the mark upon his cheek, and looking, sighed; indeed, it was the veriest ghost of a sigh, yet Barnabas heard it.

Straightaway he forgot the finger-post, forgot the world and all things in it, save her warm beauty, the red allurement of her mouth, and the witchery of her drooping lashes; therefore, he reached out his hands to her, and she saw that they were trembling.

"Cleone, oh, Cleone—look up!"

But even as he spoke, she recoiled from his touch, for plain and clear came the sound of footsteps on the road nearby.

Barnabas sighed and turned away. Yet he had gone only a little distance when he heard a voice calling him, and, swinging round, he saw Cleone standing under the finger-post.

"I wanted to give you . . . this," she said, as he came striding back, and held out a folded paper.

"It is his, my brother's . . . letter. Take it with you, it will serve to show you what a boy he is, and will tell you where to find him."

So Barnabas took the letter and thrust it into his pocket. But she yet stood before him, and now, once again, their glances avoided each other's.

"I also wanted to . . . ask you . . . about your cheek. You are quite sure it doesn't pain you . . . Mr. Bev . . ."

"Must I remind you that my name . . ."

"Are you quite sure . . . Barnabas?"

"Quite sure, yes, oh yes!" he stammered.

"Because it glows very red!" She sighed again. Though indeed she still kept her gaze averted, she added, "So will you please stoop your head a little?"

Wonderingly, Barnabas obeyed, and then, even as he did so, she leaned swiftly towards him, and for an instant her soft, warm mouth rested upon his cheek. Then, before he could stay her, she was off and away, and her flying feet had borne her out of sight.

Then Barnabas sighed, and would have followed, but the ancient finger-post barred his way with its two-arms pointing:

TO HAWKHURST. TO LONDON.

So he stopped, glanced about him to fix the hallowed place in his memory, and, obeying the directing finger, set off towards London.

On went Barnabas, swift of foot and light of heart, walking through a world of romance, with his eyes turned up to the luminous heavens.

Yet it was neither of the moon nor the stars nor the wonder thereof that he was thinking, but only of the witchery of a woman's eyes, and the thrill of a woman's lips upon his cheek; and, indeed, what should have been more natural, more right, and more altogether proper?

So it was of Lady Cleone Meredith that he

thought as he strode along the moonlit highway, and it was of her that he was thinking as he turned into that narrow by-lane where stood the Spotted Cow.

As he advanced, he espied someone standing in the shadow of one of the great trees, who, as he came nearer, stepped out into the moonlight; and then Barnabas saw that it was none other than his newly engaged valet.

The same, yet not the same, for the shabby clothes had given place to a sober, well-fitting habit, and when he took off his hat in salutation, Barnabas noticed that his hollow cheeks were clean and freshly shaved.

He was, indeed, a new man.

But now, as they faced each other, Barnabas observed something else: John Peterby's lips were compressed, and in his eyes was anxiety, which had, somehow, got into his voice when he spoke, though his tone was low and modulated.

"Sir, if you are for London tonight, we had better start at once, for the coach leaves Tenterden within the hour," said he.

"But," said Barnabas, setting his head aslant, and rubbing his chin with the argumentative air that was so very like his father, "I have ordered supper here, Peterby."

"Which—under the circumstances—I have ventured to countermand, Sir."

"Oh?" said Barnabas. "Pray what circumstances?"

"Sir, as I told you, the mail . . ."

"John Peterby, speak out—what is troubling you?"

But now, even while Peterby stood, hesitating, from the open casement of the Inn, near at hand, came the sound of a laugh; a soft, gentle, sibilant laugh, which Barnabas immediately recognised.

"Ah!" he said, clenching his fist. "I think I understand."

But as he turned towards the Inn, Peterby interposed:

"Sir," he whispered, "Sir, if ever a man meant mischief—he does. He came back an hour ago, and they have been waiting for you ever since."

"They?"

"He and the other."

"What other?"

"Sir, I don't know."

"Is he a very young man, this other?"

"Yes, Sir, he seems so. And they have been drinking together, and I've heard enough to know that they mean you harm."

But here Master Barnabas smiled with all the arrogance of youth, and shook his head.

"John Peterby," said he, "learn that the first thing I desire in my valet is obedience. Pray, stand out of my way!"

So Peterby stood aside, yet Barnabas had scarce taken a dozen strides before Clemency stood before him.

"Go back," she whispered, "go back!"

"Impossible," said Barnabas, "I have a mission to fulfil."

"Go back!" she repeated in the same tense

whisper. "You must . . . oh, you must! I've heard he has killed a man before now. . . ."

"And yet I must see and speak with his companion."

"No, no . . . ah! I pray you."

"Nay," said Barnabas. "If you will, and if need be, pray for me."

So saying, he put her gently aside, and entering the Inn, he came to the door of that room wherein he had written the letter to his father.

"I tell you I'll kill him, Dalton," said a soft, deliberate voice.

"Undoubtedly—the light's excellent! But, my dear fellow, why . . ."

"I object to him strongly, for one thing, and . . ."

The voice was hushed suddenly, as Barnabas set wide the door and stepped into the room, with Peterby at his heels.

Mr. Chichester was seated at the table with a glass beside him, but Barnabas looked past him to his companion, who sprawled on the other side of the hearth.

Young he was certainly, yet, with his first glance, Barnabas knew instinctively that this could not be the youth he sought. Nevertheless, he took off his hat and saluted him with a bow.

"Sir," said he, "pray, what might your name be?"

Instead of replying, the sleepy gentleman opened his eyes rather wider than usual, and stared at Barnabas with a growing surprise, stared at him from head to foot and down again; then, without changing his lounging attitude, he said:

"Oh, Gad, Chichester, is this the—man?"

"Yes."

"But—my dear Chit! Surely you don't propose to— This fellow, who is he? What is he? Look at his boots—oh, Gad!"

Hereupon Barnabas resumed his hat, and advancing, leaned his clenched fists on the table, and from that eminence smiled down at the speaker—that is to say, his lips curled, and his teeth gleamed in the candlelight.

"Sir," he said gently, "you will perhaps have the extreme condescension to note that my boots are strong boots, and very serviceable either for walking, or for kicking an insolent puppy."

"If I had a whip now," the gentleman sighed, "if I only had a whip, I'd whip you out of the room. Chichester—pray, look at that coat— oh, Gad!"

But Mr. Chichester had risen; and now, crossing to the door, he locked it and dropped the key into his pocket.

"As you say, the light is excellent, my dear Dalton," said he, fixing Barnabas with his unwavering stare.

"But, my dear Chit, you never mean to fight the fellow—a—a being who wears such a coat! Such boots! My dear fellow, be reasonable! Observe that hat! Good Gad! Take your cane and whip him out—positively you cannot fight this bumpkin."

"Nonetheless, I mean to shoot him—like a cur, Dalton."

Mr. Chichester drew a pistol from his pocket, and fell to examining the flint and priming with a practised eye.

"I should have preferred my regular tools, but I dare say this will do the business well enough. Pray, snuff the candles."

Now, as Barnabas listened to the soft, deliberate words, as he noted Mr. Chichester's assured air, his firm hand, his glowing eyes, and his quivering nostrils, a sudden deadly nausea came over him, and he leaned heavily upon the table.

"Sirs," he said, uncertainly, and speaking with an effort, "I have never used a pistol in my life."

"One could tell as much from his boots," murmured Mr. Dalton, snuffing the candles.

"You have another pistol, I think, Dalton? Pray, lend it to him. We will take opposite corners of the room, and fire when you give the word."

"All quite useless, Chit—this fellow won't fight."

"No," said Barnabas, thrusting his trembling hands into his pockets, "not in a corner."

Mr. Chichester shrugged his shoulders, sat down, and leaning back in his chair stared up at the pale-faced Barnabas, tapping the table-edge softly with the barrel of his weapon.

"Not in a corner—I told you so, Chit. Oh, take your cane and whip him out!"

"I mean," said Barnabas, very conscious of the betraying quaver in his voice, "I mean that, as I'm unused to shooting, the corner would be too far."

"Too far? Oh, Gad!" exclaimed Mr. Dalton. "What's this?"

"As for pistols, I have one here," continued Barnabas, "and if we must shoot, we'll do it here —across the table."

"Eh—what? Across the table! But, oh, Gad, Chichester, this is madness!" said Mr. Dalton.

"Most duels are," said Barnabas.

As he spoke he drew from his pocket the pistol he had taken from Mr. Chichester earlier in the evening, and, weapon in hand, he sank into a chair, thus facing Mr. Chichester across the table.

"But this is murder—positive murder!" cried Mr. Dalton.

"Sir," said Barnabas, "I am no duellist, as I told you, and it seems to me that this equalises our chances, for I can no more fail of hitting my man at this distance than he of shooting me dead across the width of the room.

"And, Sir, if I am to die tonight, I shall most earnestly endeavour to take Mr. Chichester with me."

There was a tremor in his voice again as he spoke, but his eye was calm, his brow serene, and his hand steady as he cocked the pistol; and leaning his elbow upon the table, he levelled the gun within six inches of Mr. Chichester's shirt-frill.

But, thereupon, Mr. Dalton sprang to his feet with a stifled oath.

"I tell you it's murder—murder!" he exclaimed, and took a quick step towards them.

"Peterby!" said Barnabas.

"Sir?" said Peterby, who had been standing rigid beside the door.

"Take my stick," said Barnabas, holding it out

towards him, but keeping his gaze upon Mr. Chichester's narrowed eyes.

"It's heavy, you'll find, and should this person presume to interfere, knock him down with it."

"Yes, Sir," said Peterby, and took the stick accordingly.

"But—oh, Gad!" exclaimed Dalton. "I tell you this can't go on!"

"Indeed, I hope not," said Barnabas, "but it is for Mr. Chichester to decide. I am ready for the count when he is."

But Mr. Chichester sat utterly still, his chin on his breast, staring at Barnabas from under his brows, one hand tightly clenched about the stock of his weapon on the table before him, the other hanging limply at his side.

So for an interval they remained thus, staring into each other's eyes, in a stillness so profound that it seemed all four men had ceased to breathe.

Then Mr. Chichester sighed faintly, dropped his eyes to the muzzle of the weapon so perilously near, glanced back at the pale, set face and unwinking eyes of he who held it, and sighed again.

"Dalton," said he, "pray, open the door, and order the chaise." Then he laid the key upon the table.

"First," said Barnabas, "I will relieve you of that encumbrance." He pointed to the pistol yet gripped in Mr. Chichester's right hand.

Without a word, Mr. Chichester rose, and, leaving the weapon upon the table, turned and walked to the window, while Mr. Dalton, having unlocked the door, hurried away to the stable-yard, and was now heard calling for the ostlers.

"Peterby," said Barnabas, "take this thing and throw it into the horse-pond. Yet—no, give it to the gentleman who just went out."

"Yes, Sir," said Peterby.

Taking up the pistol, he went out, closing the door behind him.

Mr. Chichester still lounged by the window, humming softly to himself; but as for Barnabas, he sat rigidly in his chair, staring blankly at the opposite wall, his eyes wide, his lips tense, with a gleam of moisture amidst the curls at his temples.

So the one lounged and hummed, and the other glared stonily before him, until came the grind of wheels and the stamping of hoofs. Then Mr. Chichester took up his hat and cane, and, humming still, crossed to the door and lounged out into the yard.

There came a jingle of harness, a sound of voices, the slam of a door, and the chaise rolled away down the lane, farther and farther, until the rumble of its wheels died away in the distance.

Then Barnabas laughed—a sudden, shrill laugh—and clenched his fists, and strove against the laughter, and choked, and so sank forward with his face upon his arms, as one who is very weary.

Now presently, as he sat thus, it seemed to him that someone spoke from a long way off; whereupon, in a little while, he raised his head and beheld Clemency.

"You . . . are not hurt?" she enquired anxiously.

"Hurt?" said Barnabas. "No, not hurt, Mistress Clemency, not hurt, I thank you. But I think I have grown a great deal older."

"I saw it all, through the window, and yet I ... don't know why you are alive."

"I think because I was so very much afraid," said Barnabas.

"Sir," she said, with her brown hands clasped together, "was it for ... it was for ... my sake that you ... quarrelled, and ..."

"No," said Barnabas, "it was because of another."

Now when he said this, Clemency stared at him wide-eyed, and all in a moment flushed painfully and turned away, so that Barnabas wondered.

"Good-bye!" she said suddenly, and crossed to the door.

On the threshold she paused.

"I did pray for you," she said over her shoulder.

"Ah!" said Barnabas, rising. "You prayed for me, and behold, I am alive."

"Good-bye!" she repeated, her face still averted.

"Good-bye!" said Barnabas. "And will you remember me in your prayers—sometimes?"

"My prayers! Why?"

"Because the prayers of a sweet, pure woman may come between man and evil—like a shield."

"I will," she said very softly. "Oh, I will."

And so with a swift glance she was gone.

"Now," said Barnabas to his valet, "the Tenterden coach, and London."

Chapter
Four

Some days later, in the London Inn where the coach had set them down, Barnabas and his new valet, John Peterby, sat talking one morning.

"And now, Peterby," said Barnabas, pushing his chair from the breakfast-table, "the first thing I shall require is a tailor."

"Very true, Sir."

"These clothes were good enough for the country, Peterby, but . . ."

"Exactly, Sir!" answered Peterby, bowing.

"Hum!" said Barnabas, with a quick glance. "Though mark you," he continued argumentatively, "they might be worse, Peterby; the fit is good, and the cloth is excellent. Yes, they might be a great deal worse."

"It is possible, Sir," answered Peterby, with another bow.

Hereupon, having glanced at his solemn face, Barnabas rose and surveyed himself, as well as he might, in the tarnished mirror on the wall.

"Are they so bad as all that?" he enquired.

Peterby's mouth relaxed and a twinkle dawned in his eyes.

"As garments they are serviceable, Sir," said he gravely, "but as clothes they don't exist."

"Why then," said Barnabas, "the sooner we get some that do—the better. Do you know of a good tailor?"

"I know them all, Sir."

"Who is the best—the most expensive?"

"Schultz, sir, in Clifford Street, but I shouldn't advise you to have him."

"And why not?"

"Because he *is* a tailor."

"Oh?" said Barnabas.

"I mean that the clothes he makes are all stamped with his individuality; as it were, their very excellence damns them. They are the clothes of a tailor instead of being simply a gentleman's garments."

"Hum!" said Barnabas, beginning to frown at this. "It would seem that dress can be a very profound subject, Peterby."

"Sir," answered Peterby, shaking his head, "it is a life study, and, so far as I know, there are only two people in the world who understand it aright. Beau Brummell was one, and because he was the Beau, he had London and the World of Fashion at his feet."

"And who was the other?"

Peterby took himself by the chin, and, though his mouth was solemn, the twinkle was back in his eyes as he glanced at Barnabas.

"The other, Sir," he answered, "was one who,

until yesterday, was reduced to the necessity of living upon poached rabbits."

Here Barnabas stared thoughtfully up at the ceiling.

"I remember that you told me you were the best valet in the world," he said.

"It is my earnest desire to prove it, Sir."

"And yet," said Barnabas, with his gaze still turned ceilingwards, "I would have you—even more than this, Peterby."

"More, Sir?"

"I would have you, sometimes, forget that you are only 'the best valet in the world,' and remember that you are a man, one in whom I can confide; one who has lived in this great world, and felt, and suffered, and who can, therefore, advise me.

"One I may trust in an emergency, for London is a very big place, they tell me, and my friends are few—or none—and—do you understand me, Peterby?"

"Sir," said Peterby, in an altered tone, "I think I do."

"Then—sit down, John, and let us talk."

With a murmur of thanks, Peterby drew up a chair and sat watching Barnabas with his shrewd eyes.

"You will remember," began Barnabas, staring up at the ceiling again, "that when I engaged you I told you that I intended to—hum!—to—cut a figure in the Fashionable World."

"Yes, Sir; and I told you that, after what happened in a certain wood, it was practically impossible."

"You mean because I thrashed a scoundrel?"

"I mean because you knocked down a friend of the Prince Regent."

"Is Carnaby so very powerful, Peterby?"

"Sir, he is the Prince's friend!"

"Ah!" said Barnabas.

"And since the retirement of Mr. Brummell, he and the Marquis of Jerningham have to some extent taken his place, and become the Arbiters of Fashion."

"Oh!" said Barnabas.

"And furthermore, Sir, I would warn you that he is a dangerous enemy, said to be one of the best pistol-shots in England."

"Hum," said Barnabas. "Nevertheless, I mean to begin. . . ."

"To begin, Sir?"

"At once, Peterby, and you must help."

"Me, Sir?"

"You, Peterby."

Here Peterby took himself by the chin again, and looked at Barnabas with thoughtful eyes and gloomy brow.

"Sir," he said, "the World of Fashion is a trivial world where all must appear trivial; it is a place where all must act a part, and where those who are most regarded are those who are most affected; it is a world of shams and insincerity, and it is very jealously guarded."

"So I have heard," said Barnabas, nodding.

"To gain admission you must, first of all, have money."

"Yes."

"Birth—if possible."

"Hum," said Barnabas.

"Wit and looks may be helpful, but all these are utterly useless unless you have what I may call 'the magic key.' "

"And what is that?"

"Notoriety, Sir."

"For what?"

"For anything that will serve to set you above the throng; you must be one apart, an original."

"Originality is divine!" said Barnabas.

"More or less, Sir, but it is very easily achieved. Lord Alvanly managed it with apricot-tarts; Lord Petersham with snuff-boxes; Mr. Mackinnon by his agility in climbing round drawing-rooms on the furniture; the Jockey of Norfolk by consuming a vast number of beef-steaks, one after the other.

"Sir George Cassilis, who was neither rich nor handsome nor witty, by being insolent; Sir John Lade, by dressing like a stage-coachman and driving like the devil; Sir George Skeffington by inventing a new colour and writing bad plays; and I could name you many others besides. . . ."

"Why, then, Peterby—what of Sir Mortimer Carnaby?"

"He managed it by going into the Prize Ring with Jack Fearby, the 'Young Ruffian,' and beating him in twenty-odd rounds, for one thing, and winning a cross-country race.

"But I fear, Sir," continued Peterby, "that in making him your enemy you have damned your chances at the very outset, as I told you.

"Therefore, since you honour me by asking

95

my advice, I would strive with all my power to dissuade you."

"John Peterby—why?"

"Because, in the first place, I know it to be impossible."

"I begin to think not, John."

"Why then, because it's dangerous!"

"Danger is everywhere, more or less, John!"

"And because, Sir, because you—you . . ." Peterby rose, and stood with bent head and hands outstretched, "because you gave a miserable wretch another chance to live, and therefore I— I would not see you crushed and humiliated.

"Ah, Sir! I know this London, I know those who make up the Fashionable World. Sir, it is a heartless world, cruel and shallow, where inexperience is made a mock of—generosity laughed to scorn; where he is most respected who can shoot the straightest; where men seldom stoop to quarrel, but where death is frequent nonetheless.

"And, Sir, I could not bear—I—I—wouldn't have you cut off thus!"

Peterby stopped suddenly, and his head sank lower; but as he stood thus, Barnabas rose, and coming to him took his hand into his own firm clasp.

"Thank you, John Peterby," he said. "You may be the best valet in the world—I hope you are—but I know that you are a man, and, as a man, I tell you that I have decided upon going on with the adventure."

"Then I cannot hope to dissuade you, Sir?"

"No, John!"

"Indeed, I feared not."

96

"It was for this that I came to London, and I shall begin at once."

"Very good, Sir."

"Consequently, you have a busy day before you. You see, I shall require, first of all, clothes, John; then—well, I suppose a house to live in. . . ."

"A house, Sir?"

"In a fashionable quarter, and furnished, if possible."

"A lodging, St. James's Street way, is less expensive, Sir, and more usual. I happen to know that number five, St. James's Square, is for sale."

"Good!" said Barnabas. "Buy it! A house will be more original, at least. Then there must be servants, horses, vehicles—but you will understand. . . ."

"Certainly, Sir."

"Well then, John—go and get 'em."

"Sir?" exclaimed Peterby.

"Go now, John," said Barnabas, pulling out his purse, "this very moment."

"But—but, Sir," stammered Peterby, "you will . . ."

"I shall stay here. I don't intend to stir out until you have me dressed as I should be—in 'clothes that exist,' John!"

"But you don't mean to—to entrust—everything—to—me?"

"Of course, John."

"But, Sir . . ."

"I have every confidence in your judgement, you see. Here is some money; you will want more, of course, but this will do to go on with."

But Peterby only stared from Barnabas to the money on the table and back again.

"Sir," said he at last, "this is a great deal of money. And I would remind you that we are in London, Sir, and that yesterday I was a man of no character—a . . ."

"But today you are my valet, John. So take the money and buy me whatever I require, but a tailor first of all."

Then, as one in a dream, Peterby took up the money, counted it, buttoned it into his pocket, and crossed to the door, but there he paused and turned.

"Sir," he said slowly. "I'll bring you a man who, though he is little known as yet, will be famous someday, for he is what I may term an artist in cloth. And, Sir . . ."

Here Peterby's voice grew uncertain.

"You shall find me worthy of your trust, so help me, God!"

Then he opened the door, went out, and closed it softly behind him.

But, as for Barnabas, he sat with his gaze fixed on the ceiling again, lost in reverie and very silent.

For some while Barnabas sat deep in thought. Then, suddenly, he recollected the letter in his pocket and, taking it out, read it through quickly.

*I am threatened by a GRAVE DAN-
GER.* [This doubly underlined.] *I am at my
wit's end, and only you can save me, Cleone,
you and you only. Chichester has been more*

than kind, indeed, a true friend to me! [This also underlined.] *I would that you could feel kinder towards him.*

I shall journey down to Hawkhurst to see you and shall stay about until you can contrive to meet me. Chichester may accompany me, and if he should, try to be kinder to your brother's only remaining friend.

How different are our situations! You are surrounded by every luxury, while I— yet heaven forbid I should forget my manhood and fill this letter with my woes. But if you ever loved your unfortunate brother, do not fail him in this, Cleone.

> *Your loving, but desperate,*
> *Ronald Barrymaine*

Barnabas was still staring at the letter with its scrawling signature when a carriage drew up in the Inn-yard and out of it stepped the elegant figure of the Viscount, who glimpsed Barnabas through the window, and immediately entered the Inn to greet him warmly.

Straight away they fell to talking over the events of the few days that had elapsed since they had last been together.

"By the way," said the Viscount, "talking of Carnaby, he's got the most beautiful eye you ever saw!"

"Oh?" said Barnabas, beginning to tuck in the ends of his neckerchief.

"And a devil of a split lip And his coat was nearly ripped off him; I saw it under his cape!"

"Ah?" said Barnabas, still busy with his neck-cloth.

"And naturally enough I've been racking my brain most damnably, wondering why you did it."

"It was in the wood," said Barnabas.

"So it was you, then?"

"Yes, Dick."

"But he didn't even mark you?"

"He lost his temper, Dick."

"You thrashed—Carnaby! Gad, Bev, there isn't a milling cove in England could have done it. And I'll warrant he deserved it, Bev."

"I think so," said Barnabas. "It was in the wood, Dick."

"The wood? Ah! do you mean where you . . ."

"Where I found Her lying unconscious."

"Unconscious! And with him beside her! My God, man, why didn't you kill him?"

"Because I was beside her first, Dick."

"Damn him!" exclaimed the Viscount bitterly.

"But he is your friend, Dick."

"Was, Bev, *was!* We'll make it in the past tense hereafter."

But now another man appeared from an inside room, bowed profoundly, and addressed himself to the Viscount.

"I believe," he said, smiling affably, "that I have the pleasure to behold Viscount Devenham?"

"The same, Sir," rejoined the Viscount, bowing stiffly.

"You don't remember me, perhaps, My Lord?"

The Viscount regarded the speaker stonily, and shook his head.

"No, I don't, Sir."

"My name is Digby Smivvle. And, My Lord, though my name is not familiar, I think you will remember a friend of mine. The name of my friend is Ronald Barrymaine."

The Viscount's smooth brow remained unclouded, only the glove tore on his finger; so he smiled, shook his head, and drawing it off tossed it away.

"Hum," he said, "I seem to have heard some such name—somewhere or other. Well, good-bye, my dear fellow, I shan't forget Friday next."

So saying, the Viscount shook hands, left the room, climbed into his curricle, and, with a flourish of his whip, was off and away in a moment.

"A fine young fellow, that!" exclaimed Mr. Smivvle. "High, Sir, like my friend Barrymaine; indeed you may have remarked a similarity between 'em, Sir?"

"I have never met your friend," said Barnabas.

"Ah, to be sure, a great pity! You'd like him, for Barrymaine is a cursed fine fellow—you ought to know my friend, Sir."

"I should be glad to," said Barnabas.

"Would you indeed, Sir? Stay, though; poor Barry's not himself today, under a cloud, Sir. Better wait a day, say tomorrow, or Thursday—or even Friday would do."

"Let it be Saturday," said Barnabas.

"Saturday, by all means, Sir, I'll give himself the pleasure of calling for you then."

"St. James's Square," said Barnabas, "number five."

"*Au revoir*, Sir, delighted to have had the happiness. Good-afternoon, Sir!"

With a prodigious flourish of his hat, Mr. Smivvle bowed, smiled, and swaggered off.

*   *   *

At precisely four o'clock in the afternoon of the third day, Barnabas stood before a cheval mirror in the dressing-room of his new house, surveying his reflection with a certain complacent satisfaction.

His silver-buttoned blue coat, high-waisted and cunningly rolled of collar, was a sartorial triumph; his black stockinet pantaloons, close-fitting from hip to ankle and there looped and buttoned, accentuated muscled calf and virile thigh in a manner which was somewhat disconcerting.

His snowy waistcoat was of an original fashion and cut, and his cravat was a matchless creation never before seen upon the town.

Barnabas had become a Dandy, from the crown of his curly head to his silk stockings and polished shoes, and upon the whole, he was not ill-pleased with himself.

"But they're dangerously tight, aren't they, Peterby?" he enquired suddenly, speaking his thoughts aloud.

"Tight, Sir!" repeated Mr. Barry, the tailor, reproachfully, and shaking his gentleman-like head, "impossible, Sir—with such a leg inside 'em."

"Tight, Sir?" exclaimed Peterby, from where he knelt upon the floor, having just finished looping and buttoning the garments in question. "Indeed, Sir, since you mention it, I almost fear they are a trifle too roomy. Can you bend and raise your knee, Sir?"

"Only with an effort, John."

"That settles it, Barry," said Peterby with a grim nod, "you must take them in at least a quarter of an inch."

"Take 'em in?" enquired Barnabas, aghast. "No, I'll be shot if you do—not a fraction; I can scarcely manage 'em as it is!"

Peterby shook his head in grave doubt, but at this juncture they were interrupted by a discreet knock, the door opened, and a Gentleman-in-Powder appeared.

"Are you in, Sir?" he enquired in an utterly impersonal tone.

"In?" repeated Barnabas, with a quick downwards glance at his tight nether garments. "In? In what? In where?"

"Are you at 'ome, Sir?"

"At home? Of course—can't you see that?"

"Yes, Sir," returned the Gentleman-in-Powder, the shifting of his legs showing that he was growing a little agitated.

"Then why do you ask?"

"There is a person below, Sir."

"A person? What's he like? Who is he?"

"Whiskers, Sir—name of Snivels—no card!"

"Ask him to wait. Say I'll be down at once."

"Meaning as you will—see 'im?"

"Yes," said Barnabas, "yes, of course."

The Gentleman-in-Powder bowed; his eyes

103

were calm, his brow unruffled, but his nose was more supercilious than ever as he closed the door upon it.

Mr. Smivvle, meanwhile, was standing downstairs before a mirror, apparently lost in contemplation of his whiskers, and indeed they seemed to afford him a vast degree of pleasure, for he stroked them with caressing fingers, and smiled upon them quite benevolently.

"Ah, Beverley, my boy!" he cried heartily. "Pray, forgive this horribly unseasonable visit, but —under the circumstances—I felt it my duty to— ah—to drop in on you, my dear fellow."

"What circumstances?" demanded Barnabas, a little stiffly perhaps.

"Circumstances affecting our friend Barrymaine, Sir."

"Ah?" said Barnabas, his tone changing. "What of him? Though you forget, Mr. Barrymaine and I are still strangers."

"By heaven, you are right, Sir, though— egad!—I'm only a little previous—eh, my dear fellow?"

Smiling engagingly, Mr. Smivvle followed Barnabas into a side-room, and, shutting the door with elaborate care, immediately shook his whiskers and heaved a profound sigh.

"My friend Barrymaine is low, Sir, devilishly low," he proceeded to explain. "Indeed, I'm quite distressed for the poor fellow, 'pon my soul and honour I am—for he is—in a manner of speaking —in eclipse, as it were, Sir!"

"I fear I don't understand," said Barnabas. "Do you mean he has been taken—for debt?"

104

"Precisely, my dear fellow. An old affair, ages ago, a stab in the dark! Nothing very much, in fact a mere bagatelle, only, as luck will have it, I am damnably short myself just now."

"How much is it?"

"Altogether exactly twenty-five pounds ten. An absurd sum, but all my odd cash is on the race. So I ventured here on my young friend's behalf to ask for a trifling loan—a pound—or say thirty shillings would be something."

Barnabas crossed to a cabinet, unlocked a drawer, and, taking from it a smallish bag that jingled, he began to count a certain sum upon the table.

"You said twenty-five pounds then, I think?" he said, and pushed that amount across the table.

Mr. Smivvle stared from the money to Barnabas and back again, and felt for his whiskers with fumbling fingers.

"Sir," he said, "you can't—you don't mean to —to . . ."

"Yes," said Barnabas, turning to relock the drawer.

Mr. Smivvle's hand dropped from his whiskers; indeed, for the moment he almost seemed to have forgotten their existence.

"Sir," he stammered, "I cannot allow—no indeed, Sir! Mr. Beverley, you overwhelm me. . . ."

"Debts are necessary evils," said Barnabas, "and must be paid."

Mr. Smivvle stared at Barnabas, his brow furrowed by perplexity, stared like one who is suddenly at a loss; and indeed his usual knowing air was quite gone.

Then, dropping his gaze to the money on the table, he swept it into his pocket, almost furtively, and took up his hat and cane.

"Mr. Beverley," he said, "in the name of my friend Barrymaine, I thank you, and—I—I thank you!"

He turned and went out of the room, and, as he went, he even forgot to swagger.

Barnabas crossed to a mirror, and once more fell to studying his reflection with critical eyes, in the midst of which examination he looked up to find Peterby beside him.

"Are you quite satisfied, Sir?"

"They are wonderful, John."

"The coat," said Peterby, "yes . . . the coat will pass well enough, but I have grave doubts as regards the pantaloons."

Here Barnabas drew a long sigh, in the midst of which he was interrupted by the Gentleman-in-Powder, who presented himself at the doorway with the announcement:

"Viscount Deafenem, Sir!"

Barnabas started and hurried forward, very conscious, very nervous, and for once uncertain of himself by reason of his new and unaccustomed splendour.

But the look in the Viscount's boyish eyes, his smiling nod of frank approval, and the warm clasp of his hand were vastly reassuring.

"Why, Bev, that coat's a marvel!" he exclaimed impulsively. "It is, I swear it is; turn round—so! Gad! what a fit!"

"I hoped you'd approve of it, Dick," said

106

Barnabas, a little flushed. "You see, I know very little about such things, and . . ."

"Approve of it! My dear fellow! And the cut!"

"Now—as for these—er—pantaloons, Dick. . . ?"

"Dashing, my dear fellow—devilishly dashing!"

"But rather too—too tight, don't you think?"

"Can't be, Bev, tighter the better. Have 'em made too tight to get into, and you're right. Look at mine—if I bend, I split—deuced uncomfortable, but all the mode, and a man must wear something! My fellow has the deuce of a time getting me into 'em, confound 'em. Oh, for ease, give me boots and buckskins!"

Hereupon the Viscount, having walked round Barnabas three times, and viewed him critically from every angle, nodded with an air of finality.

"Yes, they do you credit, my dear fellow—like everything else," and he cast a comprehensive glance round the luxurious apartment.

"The credit of it all rests entirely with Peterby," said Barnabas. "John, where are you?"

But Peterby had disappeared.

"You're the most incomprehensible fellow, Bev," said the Viscount, seating himself on the edge of the table and swinging his leg. "You have been a constant surprise to me ever since you found me, and now it seems you are to become a source of infernal worry and anxiety as well."

"I hope not, Dick."

"You are, though," repeated the Viscount, looking graver than ever.

"Why?"

"Because—well, because you are evidently bent upon dying young."

"How so, Dick?"

"Well, Carnaby will want a word with you, and if he doesn't shoot you, why then Chichester certainly will next time, damn him!"

"Next time?"

"Oh, I know all about your little affair with him across the table. Gad, Beverley, what a perfectly reckless fellow you are!"

"But—how do you know of this?"

"From Clemency."

"So you've seen her again, Dick?"

"Yes, of course—that is, I took Moonraker for a gallop yesterday, and happened to be that way."

"Ah!" said Barnabas.

"And she told me everything! That button you found, it was that devil Chichester's, it seems —and—and, Beverley, give me your hand! She told me how you confronted the fellow. Ha! I'll swear you had him shaking in his villain's shoes, duellist as he is."

"But," said Barnabas, as the Viscount caught his hand, "it was not altogether on Clemency's account, Dick."

"No matter, you frightened the fellow off. Oh, I know—she told me, I made her!

"She had to fight with the beast, that's how he lost his button. I tell you, if ever I get the chance at him, he or I shall get his quietus. By

God, Bev, I'm half-minded to send the brute a challenge, as it is."

"Because of Clemency, Dick?"

"Well—and why not?"

"The Earl of Bamborough's son, fighting a duel over the chambermaid of a Hedge-Tavern!"

The Viscount's handsome face grew suddenly red, and as suddenly pale again, and his eyes glowed as he fronted Barnabas across the hearth.

"Mr. Beverley," said he very quietly, "how am I to take that?"

"In friendship, Dick, for the truth of it is that—though she is as brave, as pure, as beautiful as any lady in the land, she is a chambermaid nonetheless."

"You go too far, Beverley."

"I would go farther yet for my friend, My Lord, or—for our Lady Cleone."

"Yes, I believe you would, Beverley. But you have a way of jumping to conclusions that is—devilishly disconcerting. As for Chichester, the world would be well rid of him. Talking of him, I met another rascal as I came—I mean that fellow Smivvle. Had he been here?"

"Yes."

"Begging, I suppose?"

"He borrowed some money for his friend Barrymaine."

The Viscount flushed hotly, and looked at Barnabas with a sudden frown.

"Perhaps you are unaware that that is a name I never allow spoken in my presence, Mr. Beverley."

"Indeed, My Lord, and pray, why not?"

"For one thing, because he is—what he is. . . ."

"Lady Cleone's brother."

"Half-brother, Sir, and nonetheless a—knave. I mean that he is a card-sharper, a common cheat."

"Her brother. . . ?"

"Half-brother!"

"A cheat! Are you sure?"

"Certain! I had the misfortune to make the discovery. Of course it killed him in London. All the Clubs shut their doors upon him; he was cut in the streets—it is damning to be seen in his company or even to mention his name now."

"And you—you exposed him?"

"I said I made the discovery—but I kept it to myself. The stakes were unusually high that night, and we played late. I went home with him, but Chichester was there, waiting for him.

"So I took him aside, and, in as friendly a spirit as I could, I told him of my discovery. He broke down and, while never attempting a denial, offered restitution and promised amendment.

"I gave my word to keep silent, and, on one pretext or another, the loser's money was returned. But next week the whole town hummed with the news. One night—it was at White's—he confronted me, and he gave me the lie."

The Viscount's fists were tight-clenched, and he stared down blindly at the floor.

"And, Sir, though you'll scarcely credit it, of course, I—there, before them all—I took it."

"Of course," said Barnabas, "for Her sake."

"Beverley!" exclaimed the Viscount, looking up with a sudden light in his eyes. "Oh, Bev . . ." And their hands met and gripped.

"You couldn't do anything else, Dick."

"No, Bev, no, but I'm glad you understand.

"Later it got about that I—that I was—afraid of the fellow—he's a dead shot they say, young as he is—and, well, it—it wasn't pleasant, Bev. Indeed, it got worse until I called out one of Chichester's friends and winged him—a fellow named Dalton."

"I think I've seen him," said Barnabas, nodding.

"Anyhow, Barrymaine was utterly discredited and done for—he's an outcast, and to be seen with him, or his friends, is to be damned also."

"And yet," said Barnabas, sighing and shaking his head, "I must call upon him tomorrow."

"Call upon him! Man—are you mad?"

"No, but he is Her brother, and . . ."

"And, as I tell you, he is banned by Society as a cheat!"

"And is that so great a sin, Dick?"

"Are there any—worse?"

"Oh, yes—one might kill a man in a duel or dishonour a trusting woman, or blast a man's character. Indeed, it seems to me that there are many greater sins!"

The Viscount dropped back in his chair and stared at Barnabas with horrified eyes.

"My—dear—Beverley," said he at last, "are you serious?"

"My dear Lord—of course I am."

"Then let me warn you, such ideas will never do here. Anyone holding such views will never succeed in London."

"Yet I mean to try," said Barnabas, squaring his jaw.

"But why?" said the Viscount impatiently. "Why trouble yourself about such a fellow?"

"Because She loves him, and because She asked me to help him."

"She asked you to? And do you think you can?"

"I shall try."

"How?"

"First, by freeing him from debt."

"Do you know him? Have you ever met him?"

"No, Dick, but I love his sister."

"And because of this you'd shoulder his debts? Ah, but you can't, and if you ask me why, I tell you it's because Jasper Gaunt has got him, and means to keep him.

"To my knowledge, Barrymaine has twice had the money to liquidate his debt, but Gaunt has put him off, on one pretext or another, until the money has all slipped away.

"I tell you, Bev, Jasper Gaunt has got him in his clutches, as he's got God knows how many more, as he'd get me if he could, damn him.

"Yes, Gaunt has got his claws into him, and he'll never let him go—never."

"Then I must see Jasper Gaunt as soon as may be."

* * *

That Saturday, as arranged, Mr. Smivvle took Barnabas to meet Barrymaine.

In a dingy room in a dingy house in Hatton Garden, he found the young man asleep.

Softly approaching the couch, Barnabas looked down upon the sleeper, and with the look he felt his heart leap.

A young face he saw, delicately featured, a handsome face with disdainful lips that yet drooped in pitiful weariness, a face which for all its youth was marred by the indelible traces of fierce, ungoverned passions.

And gazing down upon these features, so dissimilar in expression yet so strangely alike in their beauty and lofty pride, Barnabas felt his heart leap, because of the long lashes that curled so black against the waxen pallor of the cheek; for in that moment he almost seemed to be back in the green, morning freshness of Annersley Wood, and upon his lips there breathed a name—"Cleone."

But all at once the sleeper stirred, frowned, and started up with a bitter imprecation upon his lips that ended in a vacant stare.

"This is my friend Beverley, of whom I told you," Mr. Smivvle hastened to explain. "Mr. Barnabas Beverley—Mr. Ronald Barrymaine."

"You are welcome, Sir. Pray, be seated, Mr. Bev'ley. Indeed, my apartment might be a little more commodious, but it's all I have at p-present, and, by God, I shouldn't have even this but for Dig here! Dig's the only f-friend I have in the world, except Chichester.

113

"Of course there's Cleone, but she's only a sister after all.

"Don't know what I should do if it wasn't for Dig, d-do I, Dig? And Chichester, of course."

Barrymaine, who had crossed to the other end of the room, now turned and came towards them, swaying a little, and with a glass in his hand.

"That's the accursed part of it, debt on debt, and n-nothing to pay with. All swallowed up by that merciless blood-sucker, that . . ."

"Now, my dear fellow, calm yourself."

"Calm myself? How can I, when everything I have is his, when everything I g-get belongs to him before—curse him—even before I get it! I tell you, Dig, he's—he's draining my life away, drop by drop!

"He's g-got me down with his foot on my neck, crushing me into the mud. I say he's stamping me down into hell—damn him!"

"Sir," said Barnabas, "whom do you mean?"

"Why," cried Barrymaine, "whom should I mean but Gaunt!"

"Well then," said Barnabas, "why not free yourself?"

Ronald Barrymaine sank down upon the couch, looked at Barnabas, looked at Smivvle, drained his glass, and shook his head.

"Free of Gaunt! Hark to that, Dig. Must be dev'lishly drunk to talk such cursed f-folly! Why, I tell you again," he cried in rising passion, "that I couldn't get free of Gaunt's talons even if I had the money, and mine's all gone long ago, and half Cleone's besides; her guardian's tied up the rest.

114

"She can't touch another penny without his consent, damn him! So I'm done.

"The future? In the future is a debtors' prison that opens for me whenever Jasper Gaunt says the word.

"Hope? There can be no hope for me till Jasper Gaunt's dead and shrieking in hell-fire."

"But your debts shall be paid—if you will."

"Paid? Who—who's to pay 'em?"

"I will, on a condition."

Ronald Barrymaine sank back on the couch, staring at Barnabas with eyes wide and parted lips; then he leaned forward suddenly, sobered by surprise.

"Ah—ha!" said he, slowly. "I think I begin to understand. You have seen my—my sister."

"Yes."

"Do you know how much I owe?"

"No, but I'll pay it, on a condition."

"And your condition. Is it—Cleone?"

"No!" said Barnabas, vehemently.

"Then what is it?"

"That from this hour you give up brandy and Mr. Chichester—both evil things."

"Ha! Would you insult m-my friend?"

"Impossible! You have no friend, unless it be Mr. Smivvle here."

Now as he spoke Barnabas beheld Barrymaine's drooping head uplifted; his curving back grew straight, and a new light sprang into his eyes.

"A new life," he muttered, "to come back to it all, to out-face them all after their cursed sneers and slights! Are you sure you don't promise too much—are you sure it's not too late?"

115

"Sure and certain! But remember, the chance of salvation rests only with yourself, after all." Pointing to the half-emptied bottle, he said, "Do you agree to my conditions?"

"Yes—yes, by God, I do!"

"Then, friend, give me your hand. Today I go to see Jasper Gaunt."

So Ronald Barrymaine, standing squarely upon his feet, gave Barnabas his hand.

But even in that moment Barnabas was conscious that the door had opened softly behind him. He saw the light fade out of Barrymaine's eyes, and turning about beheld Mr. Chichester smiling at them from the threshold.

"Salvation, was it, and a new life?" he enquired.

"What?" cried Barrymaine, starting up. "Listening, were you—s-spying on me—is that your game, Chichester?"

"Now, my dear Barry," Smivvle remonstrated, "be calm. And as for you, Chichester—couldn't come at a better time! Let me introduce our friend, Mr. Beverley. . . ."

"Thank you, Smivvle, but we've met before," said Mr. Chichester drily. "Last time he posed as Rustic Virtue in homespun; today it seems he is the Good Samaritan in a flowered waistcoat, very anxiously bent on saving someone or other—conditionally, of course!"

"And what the devil has it to do with you?" cried Barrymaine, passionately.

"Why, my dear fellow, hearing that you are to be saved—on a condition—I am, naturally enough, anxious to know what the condition may be."

"Sir," said Barnabas, "my condition is merely that Mr. Barrymaine give up two evil things—namely, brandy and yourself."

Then Mr. Chichester laughed, but the scar glowed upon his pallid cheek and the lurking demon peeped out of his narrowed eyes.

"And for this our young Good Samaritan is positively eager to pay twenty thousand-odd pounds. . . ."

"As a loan," muttered Barrymaine. "It would be only a loan, and I—I should be free of Jasper Gaunt f-for good and all, damn him!"

"Ah—ah, to be sure, Ronald, our young Good Samaritan, having purchased the brother would naturally expect the sister to be grateful, my dear boy. Pah! Don't you see it, Ronald? The brother saved, the sister's gratitude gained—oh, most disinterested, young Good Samaritan!"

"Ha, by heaven, I never thought of that!" cried Barrymaine, turning upon Barnabas. "Is it Cleone—is it?"

"No," said Barnabas, folding his arms a little ostentatiously. "I seek only to be your friend in this. Think—think!—once you are free of Gaunt, life will begin afresh for you, you can hold up your head again. . . ."

"Though never in London, I fear, Ronald," added Mr. Chichester over his shoulder.

"No, no!" said Barnabas. "I tell you it would mean an ending—and a new beginning, a new life for you. . . ."

"And for Cleone!" added Mr. Chichester, again over his shoulder. "Our young, distinterested Good Samaritan knows that Cleone is too proud to permit a stranger to shoulder her brother's responsibilities. . . ."

"Proud, eh?" cried Barrymaine, leaping up in sudden boyish passion. "Well, aren't I proud? Did you ever know me to be anything else—did you?"

"Never, my dear Ronald," cried Mr. Chichester, turning at last. "You are unfortunate, but so far you have always met disaster with the fortitude of a gentleman, scorning your detractors and abominating charity."

"Ch-charity! Damn you, Chichester, d' ye think I-I'd accept any man's ch-charity? D' you think I'd ever drag Cleone to that depth—do you?"

"Never, Barrymaine, never, I swear."

"Why then—leave me alone, I can m-manage my own affairs. . . ."

"Then, Sir," said Barnabas, rising, "seeing that it really is no concern of yours after all, suppose you cease to trouble yourself any further in the matter, and allow Mr. Barrymaine to choose for himself. . . ."

"I—I have decided!" cried Barrymaine. "And I tell you . . ."

"Wait!" said Barnabas. "Mr. Chichester is going, I think. Let us wait until we are alone."

As he spoke, Barnabas took a stride towards Mr. Chichester's rigid figure, but in that moment Barrymaine snatched up the brandy bottle and sprang between them.

118

"Who are you to order my f-friends about—and in m-my own place, too! Ha! did you think you could buy me, d-did you? Did you think I-I'd sacrifice my sister—did you?

"Ha! Drunk, am I? Well, I'm sober enough to—to 'venge my honour and hers! By God, I'll kill you! Oh, let go of my arm! Damn him, I say —I'll kill him!"

But, as he struck, Mr. Smivvle caught his wrist, the bottle crashed, splintering, to the floor, and they were locked in a fierce grapple.

"Beverley—my dear fellow—go!" said Mr. Smivvle, panting. "Go—go, I can manage him."

So Barnabas turned away and went down the dingy stairs, and in his ears was the echo of the boy's drunken raving and Mr. Chichester's soft laughter.

"She said that it would be difficult and dangerous perhaps," said he to himself, "and indeed I think she was right."

Then he turned and went upon his way, lost to all but the problem he had set himself, which was this:

How he might save Ronald Barrymaine in spite of Ronald Barrymaine.

*   *   *

"As a matter of fact, I came to ask you a favour," said Barnabas to the Viscount, sometime later, seated in his drawing-room.

"Granted, my dear fellow!"

"I want you to ask your friend Captain Slingsby, whom we met the other day, to introduce me to Jasper Gaunt."

119

"Ah," said the Viscount, coming to his elbow, "you mean on behalf of that . . ."

"Of Barrymaine, yes."

"It's—it's utterly preposterous!" fumed the Viscount.

"So you said before, Dick."

"You mean to go on with it?"

"Of course!"

"You are still determined to befriend a . . ."

"More than ever, Dick."

"For Her sake?"

"For Her sake, yes, Dick. I mean to free him from Gaunt, and rescue him from Chichester—if I can."

"But, my dear fellow! Chichester is the only one who has stood by him in his disgrace, though why I can't imagine."

"I think I can tell you the reason, and in one word—Cleone!"

The Viscount started.

"What? You—think. . . ? Oh, impossible! The fellow would never have a chance; she despises him, I know."

"And fears him too, Dick."

"Fears him? Gad! What do you mean, Bev?"

"I mean that, unworthy though he may be, she idolizes her brother and for his sake would sacrifice her fortune—and herself!

"When the time comes, Chichester means to reach the sister through her love for her brother, and before he shall do that, Dick . . ."

Barnabas threw up his head and clenched his fists.

"Well, Bev?"

120

"I'll kill him, Dick."

"You mean—fight him, of course?"

"It would all be one," said Barnabas grimly.

"And how do you propose to go about the matter—to save Barrymaine?"

"I shall pay off his debts, first of all."

"And then?"

"Take him away with me."

"When?"

"Tomorrow, if possible—the sooner the better."

"And you would do all this . . ."

"For Her sake," said Barnabas softly; "besides, I promised, Dick."

"And you have seen her only once, Bev!"

"Twice, Dick."

"Gad!" said the Viscount suddenly. "Gad, Beverley, what a deuced determined fellow you are!"

"You see, I love her, Dick."

"And by the Lord, Bev, shall I tell you what I begin to think? In spite of—er—me, and the rest of 'em, in spite of everything—herself included if need be—you'll win her yet."

"And shall I tell you what I begin to think, Dick? I begin to think that you have never loved her at all."

"Eh?" cried the Viscount, staring up very suddenly. "What? Never loved—oh, Gad, Beverley! What the deuce should make you think that?"

"Clemency!" said Barnabas.

The Viscount stared, opened his mouth, shut it, and ran his fingers through his hair.

"So now," said Barnabas the persistent, "now

you know why I am anxious to meet Jasper
Gaunt. Captain Slingsby has to see him this afternoon—at least so you said, and I was wondering . . ."

The Viscount smiled and shrugged his elegant shoulders.

"Nothing easier, my dear Bev. If you're quite
sure, that is!"

*   *   *

"Here we are, Beverley!"

"Where?" Barnabas enquired.

"Kirby Street—his street. And there's the
house, his house." And Captain Slingsby pointed
his whip at a high, flat-fronted house.

It was a repellent-looking place with an iron
railing before it, and beyond this railing a deep
and narrow area where a flight of damp steps led
down to a gloomy door.

The street was seemingly a quiet one and at
this hour, deserted save for themselves and a solitary man who stood with his back to them upon
the opposite side of the way, apparently lost in
profound thought.

A very tall man he was, very upright, despite
the long white hair that showed beneath his hat,
which, like his clothes, was old and shabby, and
Barnabas noticed that his feet were bare.

This man Captain Slingsby hailed in his char-
acteristic fashion.

"Hi—you over there!" he called. "Hallo!"
The man never stirred. "O-ho! B' Gad, are you
deaf? Just come over here and hold my horses for
me, will you?"

122

The man raised his head suddenly and turned. So quickly did he turn that the countless gleaming buttons that he wore upon his coat rang a jingling chime.

Now, looking upon this strange figure, Barnabas started up, and, springing from the curricle, crossed the street and looked upon the man with a smile.

"Have you forgotten me?" asked Barnabas.

The man smiled in turn, and, sweeping off the weather-beaten hat, saluted him with an old-time bow of elaborate grace.

"Sir," he answered in his deep rich voice, "Billy Button never forgets faces. You are Barnaby Bright—Barnabas, 'till all the same. Sir, Billy Button salutes you."

"Why then," said Barnabas, rather diffidently, seeing the other's grave dignity, "will you oblige me by—by holding my friend's horses? They are rather high-spirited and nervous."

"Nervous, Sir? Ah, then they need me. Billy Button shall sing to them; horses love music, and, like trees, they are excellent listeners."

Forthwith Billy Button crossed the street with his long, stately stride, and, taking the leader's bridle, fell to soothing the horses with soft words, and to patting them with gentle, knowing hands.

"B' Gad!" exclaimed the Captain, staring. "That fellow has been used to horses—once upon a time. Poor devil!"

As he spoke he glanced from Billy Button's naked feet and threadbare clothes to his own glossy Hessians and immaculate garments, and

Barnabas saw him wince as he turned towards the door of Jasper Gaunt's house.

Now, when Barnabas would have followed, Billy Button caught him suddenly by the sleeve.

"You are not going there?" he whispered, frowning and nodding towards the house.

"Yes."

"Don't!" he whispered. "Don't! An evil place, a place of sin and shadows, of sorrow and tears, and black despair. Ah, an evil place! No place for Barnaby Bright."

Here roused by the Captain's voice, rather hoarser than usual, Barnabas turned and saw that the door of the house was open and that Captain Slingsby stood waiting for him with a slender, youthful-seeming person who smiled.

He was a pale-faced, youngish man, with colourless hair and eyes so very pale as to be almost imperceptible in the pallor of his face.

Now, even as the door closed, Barnabas could hear Billy Button singing softly to the horses.

Barnabas followed the Captain along a somewhat gloomy hall and up a narrow and winding staircase, where, halfway up, was a small landing with an alcove.

Here stood a tall, wizen-faced clock with skeleton hands and a loud, insistent, very deliberate tick. So, up more stairs to another hall, also somewhat gloomy, and a door, which the pale-eyed, smiling person obligingly opened; then, having ushered them into a handsomely furnished chamber, he disappeared.

124

The Captain crossed to the hearth and, standing before the empty grate, put up his hand and loosened his high stock with suddenly petulant fingers, rather as though he found some difficulty in breathing.

Looking at him, Barnabas saw that the debonair Slingsby had quite vanished, and in his place was another—a much older man, haggard of eye, with a face peaked and grey, and careworn beneath the brim of the jaunty hat.

"My dear Beverley," said he, "if you're ever in need—if you're ever reduced to destitution, then in heaven's name go quietly away and shoot yourself! Deuced unpleasant, of course, but it's sooner over, b' Gad!"

Then in they went through another door, and Barnabas found himself in the presence of a tall, impeccably dressed man. For a long moment Barnabas looked at him.

"You are Jasper Gaunt, I think?" said Barnabas at last.

"At your service, Sir, and you I know are Mr. Barnabas Beverley."

Jasper Gaunt bowed, and seated himself at his desk, opposite Barnabas.

His face was in shadow, for the blinds had been half-drawn to exclude the glare of the afternoon sun, and he sat, or rather lolled, in a low, deeply cushioned chair.

He studied Barnabas with eyes that were so bright and so very knowing in the ways of mankind; very still he sat, and was very quiet, waiting for Barnabas to begin.

125

Now, on the wall behind him was a long, keen-bladed dagger that glittered evilly where the light caught it.

As he sat there so very quietly and still, with his face in the shadow, it seemed to Barnabas as though he lolled there dead, with the dagger smitten sideways through his throat.

"I have come," began Barnabas at last, with an effort withdrawing his eyes from the glittering steel, "on behalf of one in whom I take an interest —a great interest."

"Yes, Mr. Beverley?"

"I have undertaken to liquidate his debts. To pay whatever he may owe, both principal and interest."

"Indeed, Mr. Beverley! And his name?"

"His name is Ronald Barrymaine."

"Ronald—Barrymaine!"

There was a pause between the words, and the smooth, soft voice had suddenly grown harsh, deep, and vibrant.

"I have made out to you a draft for more than enough as I judge to cover Mr. Barrymaine's liabilities."

"For how much exactly, Sir?"

"Twenty thousand pounds."

Jasper Gaunt stirred, sighed, and leaned forward in his chair.

"A handsome sum, Sir—a very handsome sum, but . . ."

He smiled and shook his head.

"Pray, what do you mean by 'but'?" demanded Barnabas.

"That the sum is inadequate, Sir."

126

"Twenty thousand pounds is not enough, then?"

"It is not enough, Mr. Beverley."

"Then, if you will tell me the precise amount, I will make up the deficiency."

But, here again, Jasper Gaunt smiled his slow smile and shook his head.

"That, I grieve to say, is quite impossible, Mr. Beverley."

"Why?"

"Because I make it a rule never to divulge any client's affairs to a third party; and, Sir—I never break my rules."

"Then—you refuse to tell me?"

"It is quite impossible."

There fell a silence while the wide, fearless eyes of Youth looked into the narrow, watchful eyes of Experience.

Then Barnabas rose, and began to pace to and fro across the luxurious carpet; he walked with his head bent, and the hands behind his back were tightly clenched.

Suddenly he stopped, and throwing up his head faced Jasper Gaunt, who sat lolling back in his chair again.

"I have heard," said he, "that this sum was twenty thousand pounds; but, as you say it may be more—a few pounds more, or a few hundreds more—I am therefore going to make you an offer. And my offer is this—instead of twenty thousand pounds, I will double the sum."

"Forty thousand pounds!" said Jasper Gaunt, speaking almost in a whisper.

Then all in one movement, as it seemed,

Gaunt had risen and turned to the window, and he stood there awhile with his back to the room.

"Well?" enquired Barnabas at last.

"I cannot—Sir."

"Very well," said Barnabas, "then I'll treble it. I'll pay you sixty thousand pounds! What do you say? Come—speak!"

Yet still no answer came.

Only Jasper Gaunt sank down in his chair, with his elbows on the desk, his long, white face clasped between his long, white hands, and his thin lips moved as though he had whispered to himself "sixty thousand pounds!"

"Sir, for the last time—do you accept?" demanded Barnabas.

Without glancing up, or even altering the direction of his vacant stare, and with his face still framed between his hands, Jasper Gaunt shook his head from side to side, once, twice, thrice; a gesture which there was no mistaking.

Then Barnabas fell back a step, with clenched fist upraised, but in that moment the Captain was before him and had caught his arm.

"By Gad, Beverley!" he exclaimed in a shaken voice. "Are you mad?"

"No," said Barnabas. "But I came here to buy those bills and buy them I will! If trebling it isn't enough, then . . ."

"Ah!" cried Slingsby, pointing to the usurer's distorted face. "Can't you see? Don't you guess? He can't sell! No money-lender of 'em all could resist such an offer. I tell you he daren't sell, the bills aren't his! Come away. . . ."

"Not his!" cried Barnabas. "Then whose?"

"God knows! But it's true—look at him!"

"Tell me. Tell me who holds these bills; if you have one spark of generosity—tell me!"

But Jasper Gaunt gave no sign; only the writhing fingers crept across his face, over staring eyes and twitching lips.

So, presently, Barnabas suffered Captain Slingsby to lead him from the room, down the somewhat dark and winding stairs, past the wizen-faced clock, and out into the street, already full of the glow of evening.

"It's a wonder to me," said the Captain, "yes, it's a great wonder to me that nobody has happened to kill Gaunt before now."

So the Captain frowned, sighed, and climbed up to his seat.

But when Barnabas would have followed, Billy Button touched him on the arm.

"Oh, Barnaby," said he, "oh, Barnaby Bright, look—the day is dying, the shadows are coming, in a little while it will be night. But oh, Youth, alas! I can see that the shadows have touched you already!"

And so, with a quick, upflung glance at the dismal house, he turned, waved his hand, and sped away on noiseless feet.

Chapter
Five

After this encounter, Barnabas felt a great desire to free himself from London for a while. So, saddling up his horse, he rode out into the countryside.

He had not gone far when, riding through a wood, he came upon the white-haired old man he and the Viscount had met by the river.

They greeted each other and sat down to talk. After a while Barnabas put into words the thoughts that had been in his mind for many a day.

"I was wondering if you had ever heard of a man named Chichester?"

The preacher came to his knees.

"Sir—oh, Sir—this man—Chichester, is he who stole away my daughter—who blasted her honour and my life—who . . ."

"No!"

"Yes—yes! God help me, it's true! But in her shame I love her still; oh, my pride is dead long

131

ago. I remember only that I am her father, with all a father's loving pity, and that she . . .

"And that she is the stainless maid she always was. . . ."

"Sir, oh, Sir—what do you mean?"

Barnabas saw the thin hands clasp and wring themselves even as he remembered Clemency's had done.

"I mean that she fled from pollution and found refuge among honest folk. I mean that she is alive and well, and that she lives but to feel a father's kiss of forgiveness. If you would find her, go to the Spotted Cow, near Frittenden, and ask for 'Clemency!' "

"Clemency! 'Clemency' means 'mercy.' And she called herself—Clemency!"

Then with a sudden, rapturous gesture he knelt, lifted his thin hands, and his eyes upturned to the blue heavens.

"O God!" he cried, "O Father of Mercy, I thank Thee!"

He then rose from his knees, and, turning about, set off through the golden morning towards Frittenden, and Clemency.

Barnabas, watching him go, sighed softly, then remounted his horse and rode on.

Perhaps it is not surprising that before long he found himself at a certain signpost not far from the house which Cleone had pointed out as her home some weeks before.

But, at the house, he learned that the Lady Cleone and her guardian had gone not an hour before to nearby Annersley House, where a garden-party was in progress, attended by a Duchess, no less.

With no more ado, Barnabas set off for Annersley House, but there his courage failed him a little, and instead of braving the main gates he walked round the side of the park and climbed over the wall into the garden.

Before him was a shady walk winding between clipped yews, and, following this, Barnabas presently espied a small arbour some distance away.

Now between him and this arbour was a place where four paths met. There stood an ancient sun-dial and quaintly carved seats.

And here, the sun making glory of her wondrous hair, was the Lady Cleone, with beside her the Marquis of Jerningham, to whom the Viscount had introduced him.

She sat with her elbow on her knee and her dimpled chin upon her palm.

Even from where he stood, Barnabas could see again the witchery of her dark lashes, which drooped upon the oval of her cheeks.

The Marquis was talking earnestly, gesturing now and then with his slender hand, which had quite lost its habitual languor, and stooping that he might look into the drooping beauty of her face, utterly regardless of the havoc he thus wrought upon the artful folds of his marvellous cravat.

All at once she looked up, laughed, shook her head, and, closing her fan, pointed with it towards the distant house, laughing still, but imperiously.

Hereupon the Marquis rose, albeit unwillingly, and, bowing, hurried off to obey her behest.

Then Cleone rose also, and, turning, went on slowly towards the arbour, with head drooping as one in thought.

And now, with his gaze upon that shapely back, all youthful loveliness from slender foot to the crowning glory of her hair, Barnabas sighed, and felt his heart leap as he strode after her.

But, even as he followed, oblivious of all else under heaven, he beheld another back that obtruded itself suddenly upon the scene, a broad, graceful back in a coat of fine blue cloth—a back that bore itself with a masterly swing of the shoulders.

In that instant Barnabas recognised Sir Mortimer Carnaby.

Cleone had reached the arbour, but on the threshold turned to meet Sir Mortimer's sweeping bow. She seemed to hesitate, then extended her hand, and Sir Mortimer followed her into the arbour.

My lady's cheeks were warm with rich colour, her eyes were suddenly and strangely bright as she sank into a chair, and Sir Mortimer, misinterpreting this, had caught and imprisoned her hands.

"Cleone," said he, "at last!"

The slender hands fluttered in his grasp, but his grasp was strong, and before she could stop him he was down before her on his knee, speaking passionately.

"Cleone, hear me! Nay, I will speak! All the afternoon I have tried to get a word with you, and

134

now you must hear me—you shall. And yet you know what I would say. You know I love you, and have done so from the first hour I saw you.

"And from that hour I've hungered for you, Cleone, do you hear? Ah, tell me you love me—speak to me, tell me I may hope. Speak—answer me!"

But my lady sat, staring wild-eyed at the face amidst the leaves beyond the open window, a face so handsome yet so distorted; and she saw the gleam of clenched teeth, the frowning brows, and the menacing grey eyes.

Sir Mortimer, all unconscious, had caught her listless hands to his lips, and was speaking again between his kisses.

"Speak, Cleone! You know how long I have loved you. Speak and bid me hope!

"What, silent still! Why then, give me that rose from your bosom—let it be hope's messenger, and speak for you."

But still my lady sat dumb, staring up at the face amidst the leaves. And in that moment she threw up her head rebelliously, sighed, smiled, and, uttering no word, gave Sir Mortimer the rose.

Then, even as she did so, she sprang to her feet, laughed a little tremulously, and bade Sir Mortimer, "Go! Go! Go!"

Wherefore Sir Mortimer, seeing her thus, and being wise in the ways of women, pressed the flower to his lips and so turned and strode off down the path.

When his step had died away, Cleone sank down in the chair, and spoke.

"Come out—spy!" she called.

Barnabas stepped out from the leaves.

"So much for your watching and listening!" she said.

"But he has your rose!" said Barnabas.

"And what of that?"

"And he has your promise!"

"I never spoke. . . ."

"But the rose did!"

"The rose will fade and wither. . . ."

"But it bears your promise. . . ."

"I gave no promise, and . . . and . . . oh, why did you look at me?"

"Look at you?"

"Why did you frown at me?"

"Why did you give him the rose?"

"Because it was . . . my pleasure. But why did you frown at me with eyes like . . . like a devil's?"

"I wanted to kill him—then!"

"And now?"

"Now I wish him well of his bargain, and my thanks are due to him."

"Why?"

"Because, without knowing it, he has taught me what women are."

"What do you mean?"

"I loved you, Cleone. To me you were one apart—holy, immaculate. . . ."

"Yes?" said Cleone very softly.

"And now I find you—a heartless coquette. . . ."

"Who despises eavesdroppers, and who will not be espied upon nor frowned at!"

"I did not spy upon you, or, if I did, God knows it was well intended."

"How, Sir?"

"I remember the last time we three were together in Annersley Wood."

Here my lady shivered and hid her face.

"And now you gave him the rose! Do you want the love of this man, Cleone?"

"There is only one man in all the world I despise more, and his name is—Barnabas," said she, without looking up.

"So you despise me, Cleone?"

"Yes, Barnabas."

"And I came here to tell you that I—loved you—and to ask you to be my wife. . . ."

"And you looked at me with devil's eyes. . . ."

"Because you were mine, and because he . . ."

"Yours, Barnabas? I never said so."

"Because I loved you—worshipped you, and because . . ."

"Because you were jealous, Barnabas!"

"Because I would have my wife immaculate. . . ."

"But I am not your wife."

"No," said Barnabas, frowning; "she must be immaculate."

Now when he said this he heard her draw a long, quivering sigh, and with the sigh she rose to her feet and faced him.

Her eyes were wide and very bright and the fan she held snapped suddenly in her white fingers.

"Sir," she said very softly, "I whipped you

137

once. If I had a whip now, your cheek should burn again."

"But I should not want you to kiss it—this time!" said Barnabas.

"Yes," she said, in the same soft voice, "I despise you for a creeping spy, a fool, a coward —a maligner of women. Oh, go away—pray go! Leave me, lest I stifle."

But now, seeing the flaming scorn of him in her eyes, in the passionate quiver of her hands, he grew afraid, cowed by her very womanhood.

"In-indeed," he stammered, "you are unjust. I—I did not mean . . ."

"Go!" said she, as cold as ice. "Get back over the wall. Go away before I call for help."

Then Barnabas laughed softly, savagely, and, reaching out, caught her up in his arms and crushed her to him.

"Call if you will, Cleone, but listen first! I said to you that my wife should come to me immaculate—fortune's spoilt darling though she be —petted, wooed, pampered though she is—and, by God, so you shall!

"For I love you, Cleone, and if I live, I will someday call you 'wife' in spite of all your lovers, and all the roses that ever bloomed. Now, Cleone —call them if you will."

So saying, he set her down and freed her from his embrace. But my lady, leaning breathlessly in the doorway, only looked at him once, frowning a little, panting a little—a long, wondering look beneath her lashes, and then turned and was gone among the leaves.

Then Barnabas picked up the broken fan very tenderly and put it into his bosom-pocket, and so sank down in the chair, his chin propped up on his fist, frowning blackly at the glory of the afternoon.

"Very dramatic, Sir! Though indeed you missed an opportunity—and gracious heavens, how he frowns!"

Barnabas started, and glancing up beheld an ancient lady, very small and very upright.

"Madam," said Barnabas, frowning in surprise, "you were listening?"

"At the back of the arbour," she nodded, "with my ear at the panelling . . . I am sometimes a little deaf, you see."

"You mean that you were actually prying?"

"And I enjoyed it all very much, especially your 'immaculate' speech, which was very heroic, but perfectly ridiculous, of course. Indeed, you are a dreadfully young, young Sir, I fear.

"In the future, I warn you, do not tell a woman too often how much you respect her, or she'll begin to think you don't love her at all. To be over-respectful doesn't sit well on a lover, and 'tis most unfair and very trying to the lady, poor soul!"

"To harken to a private conversation doesn't sit well on a lady, Madam, or an honourable woman."

"No, indeed, young Sir. But then, you see, I'm neither. I'm only a Duchess, and a very old one at that. But all the world loves a lover, and so do I. As soon as ever I saw you I knew you for a lover of the all-or-nothing type.

"That was why I followed you, and why I watched and listened; and I grieve to say I didn't find you as deliciously brutal as I had hoped."

"Brutal, Madam? Indeed I . . ."

"Of course! When you snatched her up in your arms, and I'll admit you did it very well—but when you had her there, you should have covered her with burning kisses, and with an oath after each. Girls like Cleone need a little brutality."

She smiled and added:

"So Cleone has actually refused poor Jerningham—the yellow-maned minx!"

"But," said Barnabas, frowning and shaking his head, "Sir Mortimer Carnaby has her promise!"

"Fiddlesticks!"

"She gave him the rose!" said Barnabas, between set teeth.

The Duchess tittered.

"Dear heart! How tragic you are! Suppose she did, what then? And besides . . . hum! This time it is young D'arcy, it seems . . . callow, pink, and quite harmless."

"Madam?" said Barnabas, wondering.

"Over there . . . behind the marble faun . . . there she is!"

Following the direction of the Duchess's pointing fan, Barnabas saw Cleone, sure enough. Her eyes were drooped demurely before the ardent gaze of the handsome, pink-cheeked young soldier who stood before her, and in her white fingers she held a single red rose.

Now all at once (and as though utterly unconscious of the burning, watchful eyes of Barnabas), she lifted the rose to her lips and, smiling, gave it into the young soldier's eager hand. Then they strolled away, his epaulette very near the gleaming curls at her temple.

"I'm going—I cannot bear—any more!"

"First tell me why weren't you formally presented to me with the other guests."

"Because I'm not a guest, Madam."

"Sir—explain yourself."

"I mean that I came over the wall, Madam."

"The wall! Climbed over? Dear heaven! The monstrous audacity of the man! You came to see Cleone, of course?"

"Yes, Madam."

"Ah, very right . . . very proper! I remember I had a lover . . . in the remote ages, of course . . . who used to climb . . . ah, well . . . no matter!"

She sighed, then continued:

"Well, you came to see Cleone, you found her . . . and nicely you have behaved to each other when you met! Youth is always so dreadfully tragic! But then, what would love be without a little tragedy?

"How you must adore each other! Oh, Youth, Youth! And there's Sir George Annersley with Jerningham and Major Piper. You must meet them."

"No, indeed—I . . ." stammered Barnabas, who had met Jerningham with the Viscount many times of late.

"Sir," said the Duchess, button-holing him again. "I insist! Oh, Sir George . . . gentlemen!" she called.

Hereupon three lounging figures turned simultaneously and came hurrying towards them.

"Deuce take me—it's Beverley!" exclaimed the Marquis, and held out his hand.

"What, you know each other?" the Duchess enquired.

"Mr. Beverley is riding in the steeplechase on the fifteenth," the Marquis answered.

"And he never told me a word of it!" exclaimed the Duchess. "Of course all my money is on Jerningham . . . though Moonraker carries the odds; but I must have a hundred or two on Mr. Beverley, for friendship's sake."

"Friendship!" exclaimed the Marquis.

"Yes, gentlemen," the Duchess smiled, "this is a friend of mine who . . . dropped in on me, as it were, quite unexpectedly . . . over the wall, in fact. My friend Mr. Beverley, Sir George Annersley. Mr. Beverley, Major Piper."

"A friend of Her Grace is always welcome here, Sir," said Sir George.

"Delighted!" The Major smiled, saluting him in turn.

"Marquis, your arm. Mr. Beverley, yours. Now, Sir George, show us the way to the marquee; I'm dying for a dish of tea, I vow I am!"

Thus, beneath the protecting wing of a Duchess was Barnabas given his first taste of Quality and Blood.

He entered a world of silks and satins and glittering gems, of broadcloth and fine line, a world where the friendship of a Duchess may transform a nobody into a *somebody*.

In a word, Barnabas had arrived—even into the World of Fashion.

"Pray," said Barnabas suddenly, at tea, "pray, where did you get that rose, Marquis?"

"This? Oh, she gave it to me."

"Cleone? But—I thought she'd refused you."

"Oh, yes—so she did; but that's just like Cleone, frowning one moment, smiling the next —April, you know."

"And did she—kiss it first?"

"Kiss it? Why, deuce take me, now that I come to think of it, so she did, at least. What now, Barnaby?"

"I'm going!" said Barnabas.

He turned to the Duchess.

"Madam, I am about to leave, and—with your permission—I . . ."

"You have my permission to sit here beside me, Sir. Why, here comes Sir Mortimer Carnaby. . . . Heavens, how handsome he is! And you thrashed him, I think. Oh, I know all about it, Sir, and I know why!"

"Then," said Barnabas, "you'll know he deserved it, Madam!"

"Mm! Have you met him since?"

"No indeed, nor have I any desire to!"

"Oh, but you must."

She turned to Carnaby and said:

"My dear Sir Mortimer, I don't think you are acquainted with my friend Mr. Beverley. Mr. Beverley, Sir Mortimer Carnaby."

"Honoured, Sir," said Sir Mortimer, as they bowed.

"I see you wear Cleone's favour; you've been admitted to the Order of the Rose, like all the others."

The Duchess tittered.

"Others, Your Grace! What others?"

"Oh, Sir, there's Jerningham," she said, "and young Denton, and Snelgrove and Ensign D'arcy, and hosts besides. Lud, Sir Mortimer, where are your eyes? Look there! and there! and there again!"

And with little darting movements of her fan, she indicated certain young gentlemen, who strolled to and fro upon the lawn; now, in the lapel of each of their coats was a single red rose.

"There's safety in numbers, and Cleone was always cautious!" said the Duchess and tittered again.

Sir Mortimer glanced from those blooms to the flower in his own coat, and his cheek grew darkly red, and his mouth took on a cruel look.

"Ah, Duchess," he smiled, "it seems our fair Cleone has an original idea of humour—very quaint, upon my soul!"

He laughed, and bowing, turned away.

"Now . . . watch!" said the Duchess. "There!"

As she spoke, Sir Mortimer paused, and with a sudden, fierce gesture tore the rose from his coat and tossed it away.

"Now, really," said the Duchess, leaning back and fanning herself placidly, "I think that was vastly clever of me; you should be grateful, Sir, and so should Cleone. . . . Hush . . . here she comes, at last. Ssh! behind us . . . on the other side of the hedge . . . clever minx!"

She rose and left him to speak to Sir George.

"So that is the reason," said Cleone's clear

144

voice, speaking within a yard of them, "that is why you dislike Mr. Beverley?"

"Yes, and because of his presumption!" said a second voice.

"His presumption in what, Mr. Chichester?"

"In his determined pursuit of you."

"Is he in pursuit of me?"

"Cleone, you know he is!"

"But how do you happen to know?"

"From his persecution of poor Ronald, for one thing. He found his way to Ronald's wretched lodging, and tempted the poor fellow with his gold, indeed almost commanded Ronald to allow him to pay off his debts. . . ."

"But Ronald refused, of course?"

"And yet, Cleone, when your unfortunate brother refused his money—this utter stranger, this Good Samaritan—actually went behind Ronald's back and offered to buy up his debts! Such a thing might be done by father for son, or brother for brother, but why should any man do so much for an utter stranger. . . ?"

"Either because he is very base or very noble!" said Cleone.

"Noble! No man would part with a fortune to benefit a stranger—unless he had a powerful motive!"

"Well?" said Cleone softly.

"Well, Cleone, I happen to know that motive is—yourself. Oh, it is all very simple, Cleone, and very clumsy."

He smiled smugly.

"In the guise of Good Samaritan," he went on, "this stranger buys the debts of the brother, trusting to the gratitude of the sister. He knows your pride, Cleone, so he would buy your brother and put you under lasting obligation to himself. The scheme is a little coarse, and very clumsy—but then, he is young."

"And you say . . . he tried to pay these debts . . . without Ronald's knowledge! Are you sure . . . quite sure?" asked Cleone.

"Quite! And I know also that when Ronald's creditor refused, he actually offered to double—even to treble the sum! But indeed, you would be cheap at sixty thousand pounds, Cleone!"

"Oh . . . hateful! Pray, find my guardian and bring him to me."

"First tell me I may see you again, Cleone, before I leave for London?"

"Yes," said Cleone, after a momentary hesitation. With a bow Mr. Chichester left.

Then Barnabas sighed, a long, bitter sigh, and looking up saw Cleone standing before him.

"So you meant to buy me, Sir . . . as you would a horse or dog?"

"No," said Barnabas, speaking almost humbly.

"It would have been the same thing, Sir. You would have put upon me an obligation I could never, never have hoped to repay."

"Yes, I see my error now. I acted for the best, but I am a fool, and a clumsy one, it seems. I meant to serve you, to fulfil the mission you gave me, and I blundered because I am very ignorant. If you can forgive me, do so."

"But why . . . why did you do it?"

146

"I meant to free him from the debt which is crushing him down and unmanning him."

"But . . . oh, don't you see . . . he would still be in debt to you?"

"I had forgotten that!"

"And so you went and offered to buy up his debts for three times the proper sum?"

"I would have paid whatever was asked, because I promised you to help him," answered Barnabas, staring at the ground again.

"You must be . . . very rich?" said Cleone, enquiringly, stealing another look at him.

"I am."

"And . . . supposing you had taken over the debt—who did you think would ever repay you?"

"It never occurred to me."

"And you would have done all this for a . . . stranger?"

"No, but because of the promise I gave."

"To me?"

"Yes, but, as God sees me, I would have looked for no recompense at your hands."

"Never?"

"Unless I—I had dreamt it possible that you could ever have loved me."

Barnabas was actually stammering, and he was looking at her—pleading, she knew, but this time my lady kept her face averted.

And after a full minute my lady spoke, with her face still averted.

"The moon is at the full tonight, I think?"

"Yes."

"Are you riding back to London tonight?"

147

"Yes."

"Do you remember the madman we met at Oakshott's Barn? Do you remember what he prophesied . . . about . . . an 'orbèd moon' and 'Barnaby Bright'?"

"Yes, yes, he said we should meet again at Barnaby Bright, under an orbèd moon!"

"Do you remember the old finger-post on the Hawkhurst road?"

"Yes, do you mean—Oh, Cleone . . ."

"Here comes the Duchess with my guardian . . . hush! At nine o'clock, Sir."

Chapter
Six

It was evening, with the promise of a glorious night, when Barnabas strolled along the road, thinking only of Cleone, of the subtle charm of her voice, of the dimple in her chin, of her small, proud feet, and of her thousand sly bewitchments; at the memory of her glowing beauty, his flesh thrilled and his breath caught.

Suddenly he heard a sound from the shadows, and looking closer he saw a gleam of silver hair, and stooping, touched the prostrate figure. The heavy head was raised, and the mournful voice said:

"Is it you, young Sir? You will grieve, I think, to learn that my atonement is not complete, my pilgrimage unfinished. I must wander the roads again, for, Sir—Clemency is gone, my Beatrix is vanished. I am a day too late! Only one day, Sir, and there lies the bitterness."

"Gone?"

"She left the place yesterday, very early in

149

the morning—fled away, none know wither—I am too late!"

"But why—why did she go?"

"Young Sir, the answer is simple, the man Chichester had discovered her refuge. She was afraid!"

"Where are you going?"

"Sir, my trust is in God, therefore I take to the road again."

"To search for her?"

"To preach for her. And when I have preached sufficiently, God will bring me to her. You are for London, I fancy, young Sir? Then we part here.

"But before I bid you God-speed, I would know your name—mine is Darville—Ralph Darville."

"And mind, Sir, is Barnabas—Beverley."

"Beverley!" said the Preacher, glancing up quickly, "of Ashleydown?"

"Sir," said Barnabas, "surely they are all dead?"

"True, true!" The Preacher nodded. "The name is extinct. That is how the man—Chichester —came into the inheritance. I knew the family well, years ago.

"The brothers died abroad, Robert, the elder, with his regiment in the Peninsular, Francis in battle at sea, and Joan—like my poor Beatrix, was unhappy and ran away, but she was never heard of again."

"And her name was Joan?" said Barnabas slowly. "Joan Beverley?"

"Yes."

"Sir, Joan Beverley was my mother! I took her name—Beverley—for a reason."

"Your mother! Ah, I understand it now. You are greatly like her, at times; it was the resemblance that puzzled me before. But, Sir—if Joan Beverley was your mother, why then . . ."

"Then, Chichester has no right to the property?"

"No!"

"And I have?"

"If you can prove your descent."

"Yes, but to whom?"

"You must seek out a Mr. Gregory Dyke, of Lincoln's Inn; he is the Lawyer who administered the estate. . . ."

"Stay, let me write it down."

"And now, young Sir," said the Preacher, when he had answered all the eager questions of Barnabas as fully as he might, "you know I have small cause to love the man Chichester, but remember, you are rich already, and if you take this inheritance also—he will be destitute."

"Sir," said Barnabas, frowning, "better one destitute and starving than that many should be wretched, surely."

So they clasped hands; then, sighing, the Preacher turned and plodded on his lonely way.

But Barnabas stood, his fists clenched, his mouth set, until he was roused by a very small sound like the jingle of distant spurs. Barnabas lifted his head and glanced about him, but, seeing no one, presently went his way, slow of foot and very thoughtful.

At nine o'clock exactly, Barnabas stepped

from the shadows by the signpost to meet Cleone.

"I began to fear you wouldn't come," he said.

"But tonight is Barnaby Bright, and the prophecy must be fulfilled, Sir. And ... oh, how wonderful the moon is!"

Now, lifting her head to look at it, her hood must needs take occasion to slip back upon her shoulders, as if eager to reveal her loveliness, the high beauty of her face, the smooth round column of her throat, and the shining wonder of her hair.

"Cleone, how beautiful you are. Cleone, when will you marry me?"

"You are very impetuous, I think," she said, and sighed.

"I—love you," said Barnabas, "not only for your beauty but because you are Cleone, and there is no one else in the world like you. But, because I love you so much, it—it is very hard to tell you of it. If I could only put it into fine-sounding phrases ..."

"Don't!" said my lady quickly, and she laid a slender (though very imperious) finger upon his lips.

"Why?" Barnabas enquired, very properly kissing the finger and holding it there.

"Because I grow tired of fine phrases and empty compliments, and because, Sir ..."

"Have you forgotten that my name is Barnabas?" he demanded.

He kissed the captive finger again, whereupon it struggled, though very feebly to be sure.

"And because, Barnabas, you would be breaking your word."

152

"How?"

"You must only tell me that when 'the sun is shining, and within call' . . . have you forgotten your own words so soon?"

Now, as she spoke, Barnabas beheld the dimple, that most elusive dimple, which came and went and came again, beside the scarlet lure of her mouth.

And now he drew her nearer, until he could look, for a moment, into the depths of her eyes.

But here, seeing the glowing intensity of his gaze, she became aware of the strong, compelling arm about her, and felt the quiver of the hand that held her own.

Lo! in that instant my lady, with her sly bewitchments, her coquettish airs and graces, was gone, and in her place was the maid, quick-breathing, blushing, and trembling all in a moment.

"Ah, no!" she pleaded. "Barnabas, no!"

And in that moment he caught her close, and thus, for the first time, their lips met.

"Cleone!"

"Oh!" she whispered. "Why . . . why did you?"

"Because I love you!"

"No other man ever dared to . . ."

"Heaven be praised!"

"Upon . . . the mouth!" she added, her face still hidden.

"Then I have set my seal upon it."

"And now . . . am I . . . immaculate?"

"Oh—forgive me!"

"No!"

"Look at me."

153

"No!"

"Are you angry?"

"Yes, I think I am, Barnabas . . . oh, very!"

"Forgive me!"

"First, am I heartless and a coquette?"

"No, indeed no! Oh, Cleone, is it possible you could learn to love me, in time?"

"I . . . I didn't come to answer idle questions, Sir," said my lady, suddenly demure. "It must be nearly half-past nine . . . I must go. I forgot to tell you . . . Mr. Chichester is coming to meet me to-night. . . ."

"Chichester—here!"

"At a quarter to ten, Barnabas; that is why I must go at half-past nine. . . . Barnabas, stop! Oh, Barnabas, you're crushing me! Not again, Sir . . . I forbid you . . . please, Barnabas!"

So Barnabas loosened her regretfully, and stood watching while she patted her shining hair into order.

"Ah! Now you're frowning again, and it's nearly time for me to go, and I haven't had a chance to mention what I came for, which of course is all your fault, Barnabas. Today I received a letter from Ronald.

"Here is the letter, will you read it? You see, I have no one who will talk to me about poor Ronald, no one seems to have any pity for him."

"But you will always have me, Cleone!"

"Always, Barnabas?"

"Always."

So Barnabas took Ronald Barrymaine's letter, and opening it he read as follows:

Dearest of Sisters,

I was unable to keep the appointment I begged for in my last, owing to a sudden indisposition, and, though better now, I am still ailing.

Chichester has offered me an asylum at his country place near Headcorn, where I hope to regain something of my wonted health. But for Chichester I tremble to think what would have been my fate long before this.

Ah, Cleone! Chichester's devotion to you is touching; such patient adoration must, in time, meet with its reward. Cleone, give my friend the answer he seeks, the answer he has sought of you already, the answer which to your despairing brother means more than you can ever guess, the answer whereby you can fulfil the promise you gave our dying mother to help

Your unfortunate brother,
Ronald Barrymaine

Now, as he finished reading, Barnabas frowned, tore the letter across in sudden fury, and looked up to find Cleone frowning also.

"You have torn my letter!"

"It is the letter of a coward and weakling! He would sell you to a . . ."

"Mr. Chichester is my brother's friend. And poor Ronald is sick. . . ."

"With brandy!"

"Oh . . . not that! Not that!"

"Didn't you know?"

"I only dreaded it. His father died of it. Oh,

155

Barnabas! There is no one else who will help him,
save him from that! You will try, won't you?"

"Yes. No one can help a man against his will,
but I'll try. And I ask you to remember that if I
succeed or not, I shall never expect any recompense from you, never!"

"Unless, Barnabas . . ."

"Unless—oh, Cleone, unless you should—
someday learn to—love me—just a little, Cleone?"

"Would just a little satisfy you?"

"No, no, I want you all. Oh, Cleone, will you
marry me?"

"You are very persistent, Sir, and I must go."

"Not yet—pray, not yet."

"Please, Barnabas. I would not care to see
Mr. Chichester tonight."

"No, you must go. But first—will you. . . ?"

"Not again, Barnabas!"

And she gave him her two hands, so he
stooped and kissed them instead. Then she turned
and left him standing bare-headed under the finger-
post.

But when she had gone but a little way she
paused and said to him over her shoulders:

"Will you write to me . . . sometimes?"

"Oh—may I?"

"Please, Barnabas . . . to tell me of . . . my
brother."

"And when can I see you again?"

"Ah! Who can tell?" she answered.

And so, smiling a little, blushing a little, she
hastened away.

Now when she was gone, Barnabas stooped,
very reverently, and pressed his lips to the ancient

finger-post, on that spot where her head had rested, and then he sighed, and turned towards his great black horse.

But, even as he did so, he heard again that soft sound that was like the faint jingle of spurs, the leaves of the hedge rustled, and out into the moonlight stepped a tall figure, wild of aspect, bare-headed, and bare of foot.

One who wore his coat wrong-side out, and who, laying his hand upon his bosom, bowed in stately fashion, once to the moon and once to him.

"Do you remember, Barnaby Bright, how I foretold we should meet again, under an orbèd moon? Was I not right? She's fair, Barnaby, and passing fair, and very proud; but all good, beautiful women are proud and hard in the winning—oh, I know! Billy Button knows!

"So I followed you, Barnaby Bright, I came to warn you of the shadow. It grows blacker every day—back there in the great city, waiting for you, Barnaby Bright, to smother you—to quench hope, and light, and life itself.

"But I shall be there—and She. A-ha! She shall forget all things then—even her pride. Shadows have their uses, Barnaby, even the blackest.

"I came a long way, oh, I followed you. But poor Billy is never weary, the Wise Ones bear him up in their arms sometimes. So I followed you—and another, also, though he didn't know it. O-ho! Would you see me conjure you a spirit from the leaves yonder? Ah! but an evil spirit, this! Shall I? Watch now!"

So saying, the speaker flung up his long arms,

and with his gaze fixed upon a certain part of the hedge, he lifted his voice and said:

"O-ho, lurking spirit among the shadows! Ho! come forth, I summon ye. The dew is thick amidst the leaves, and dew is an evil thing for purple and fine linen. O-ho, stand forth, I bid ye."

There followed a moment's utter silence, then another rustle amidst the leaves, and Mr. Chichester stepped out from the shadows.

"Ah, Sir," said Barnabas, consulting his watch, "you are just twenty-three minutes before your time. Nevertheless, you are, I think, too late."

Mr. Chichester glanced at Barnabas from head to foot, and, observing his smile, Barnabas clenched his fists.

"Too late, Sir?" repeated Mr. Chichester softly, shaking his head. "No—indeed, I think not. Howbeit, there are times and occasions when solitude appeals to me, and this is one."

"First, Sir," said Barnabas, bowing with aggressive politeness, "first, I humbly beg leave to speak with you, to . . ."

"Sir," said Mr. Chichester, "Sir, I have no desire for your speeches; they, like yourself, I find a little trying, and vastly uninteresting. I bid you good-night, Sir, and a pleasant ride."

"Nonetheless, Sir," said Barnabas, beginning to smile, "I fear I must inflict myself upon you a moment longer, to warn you that I . . ."

"To warn me? Again? Oh, Sir, I grow weary of your warnings, I do indeed! Pray, go away and warn somebody else. Pray, go and let me stare upon the moon and twiddle my thumbs until . . ."

"If it is the Lady Cleone you wait for, she is gone!"

"Ah!" Mr. Chichester sighed, viewing Barnabas through narrowed eyes. "Gone, you say? But then, young Sir, Cleone is one of your tempting, warm, delicious creatures. Cleone is a skilled coquette to whom all men are—men. Tonight it is you; tomorrow . . . ?"

Mr. Chichester's right hand vanished into the bosom of his coat as Barnabas strode forward, but, on the instant, Billy Button was between them.

"Stay, My Lord!" he cried. "Look upon this face, 'tis the face of my friend Barnaby Bright, but, My Lord, it is also the face of Joan's son. You heard tell of Joan, poor Joan who was unhappy, and ran away, and got lost—you'll mind Joan Beverley?"

Now, in the pause that followed, as Mr. Chichester gazed at Barnabas, his narrowed eyes opened, little by little his compressed lips grew slowly loose, and the tasselled cane slipped from his fingers, and lay all neglected.

"Sir," said Barnabas at last, "this is what I would have told you. I am the lawful son of Joan Beverley, whose maiden name I took for—a purpose. I have but to prove my claim and I can dispossess you of the inheritance you hold, which is mine by right. But, Sir, I have enough for my needs, and I am therefore prepared to forego my just claim—on a condition."

Mr. Chichester neither spoke nor moved.

"My condition," Barnabas continued, "is this:

"That, from this hour, you loose whatever hold you have upon Ronald Barrymaine, that you have no further communication with him, either by word or letter.

"Failing this, I institute proceedings at once, and will dispossess you as soon as may be.

"Sir, you have heard my condition, it is for you to answer."

But, as he ended, Billy Button pointed a shaking finger downwards at the grass midway between them, and spoke.

"Look!" he whispered. "Look! Do you not see it, bubbling so dark—down there among the grass. Ah! It reaches your feet, Barnaby Bright. But look yonder! It rises to his heart, look!" And with a sudden, wild gesture he pointed to Chichester's rigid figure.

"Blood!" he cried. "Blood! Cover it up! Oh, hide it—hide it!"

Then, turning about, Billy sped away, his muffled buttons jingling faintly as he went, and so was presently gone.

Then Barnabas loosed his horse and mounted, and, with never a glance nor word to the silent figure beneath the finger-post, galloped away to London.

But Mr. Chichester stood very still, and stared long upon the moon, with his right hand still hidden in the breast of his coat. The vivid mark glowed and glowed upon the pallor of his cheek.

*   *   *

Some days later, Barnabas sat in the George Inn, writing once more to his father. Pausing for a moment in his labours, he became aware that someone had entered the room, and, turning, he beheld Mr. Chichester.

"Sir," he said, "I would remind you that the last time we met, you warned me—indeed, you have a weakness for warning people, it seems—you also threatened me that unless I agreed to—certain conditions—you would dispossess me of my inheritance. . . ."

"And I repeat it."

"Oh, Sir, save your breath and listen," Mr. Chichester smiled, "for let me tell you, threats beget threats, and warnings, warnings! Here is one, which I venture to think you will heed!"

So saying, he unfolded a letter and laid it upon the table.

Barnabas glanced at it, hesitated, then stooped, and read as follows:

> *Dear Lady Cleone,*
> *I write this to warn you that the person calling himself Mr. Beverley, and posing as a gentleman of wealth and breeding, is, in reality, nothing better than a rich vulgarian, one Barnabas Barty, son of a country Inn-keeper. The truth of which shall be proved to your complete satisfaction whenever you will, by*
> *Yours always humbly to command,*
> *Wilfred Chichester*

Barnabas sank down into a chair, and, leaning his elbows upon the table, hid his face between his hands; seeing which, Mr. Chichester laughed softly, and, taking up the letter, turned to the door.

"Sir, as I mentioned before, threats beget threats. I tell you, if you presume to interfere with me again in any way—or with my future plans in any way—then in that same hour, Cleone shall know you for the impudent imposter you are!"

So Mr. Chichester laughed again, and laid his hand upon the latch of the door. But Barnabas sat rigidly, and did not move or lift his heavy head even when the door opened and closed and he knew he was alone.

"Is there anything I can get you, Sir," said a waiter, entering a moment later.

"Yes," said Barnabas heavily. "My hat."

In no time, it seemed, he was on his way back to Annersley.

To his immense surprise, the first person he saw on dismounting at the old signpost was the Duchess, who did not seem in the least startled to see him.

"Mr. Beverley," she said in welcome, "I'm glad to see you are here so well to time."

"To time, Madam?"

"Yes. I bet Cleone an Indian shawl against a pair of beaded mittens that you would be here, to-day, before ten o'clock. So you see, you are hours before your time, and the mittens are mine.

"Talking of Cleone, Sir, she's in the orchard. She's also in a shocking temper . . . indeed, quite cattish, so you'd better stay here and talk to me."

"Willingly. You see, Madam, I need your help, your advice," said Barnabas gravely. "To-day I tried to write to Cleone, to tell her everything, but I couldn't."

162

"So you decided to come and tell me first, which was very nice of you. Well, Sir, I'm listening."

"First then, you must know that my real name is Barty. Beverley was my mother's name. She was Joan Beverley."

"Joan. Joan Beverley? Why . . . yes, I think I remember her, and the talk there was. Joan? Ah yes, to be sure . . . very handsome, and she . . . disappeared."

"She became the honourable wife of my father, John Barty, the celebrated pugilist and ex-Champion of England, now Landlord of a village Inn," said Barnabas, speaking all in a breath, but maintaining his steadfast gaze.

"Eh?" cried the Duchess, and rose to her feet with astonishing ease for one of her years. "Eh, Sir, an Inn-keeper! And your mother actually married him?"

The Duchess shivered.

"Yes, Madam. I am their lawful son."

"Dreadful! Frightful! An Inn-keeper's son! Oh, shocking!"

"Ah, so you scorn me already?"

"Of course."

"For being an Inn-keeper's son?"

"For telling of it!"

"And yet I think Barnabas Barty is a better man than Barnabas Beverley, and a more worthy lover. Indeed, I know he is. And, as Barnabas Barty, I bid Your Grace good-bye!"

"Where are you going?"

"To the village Inn, Madam, my proper place,

it seems. But tomorrow morning, unless you have told Cleone, I shall."

"Why?"

"Because I love her. Because I, therefore, hate deceit, and because I . . ."

"Well?"

"And because Mr. Chichester knows already."

"Ah! You mean that he has forced your hand, Sir, and now you would make the best of it. . . ."

"I mean that he has opened my eyes, Madam."

"And tomorrow you will tell Cleone?"

"Yes."

"And your friends—the Marquis, Viscount Devenham, and the rest?"

"They will, I expect, turn their gentlemanly backs upon me—as you yourself have done. So, Madam, I thank you for your past kindness, and bid you good-bye!"

"Stop, Sir!"

"Of what avail, Madam?" said Barnabas, sighing as he turned away.

"Barnabas," said the Duchess, very softly, "oh, dear me, I'm glad you told me, oh very! I hoped you would!"

"Hoped? Why—why, Madam, you—then you knew?"

"All about it, of course! Oh, you needn't stare, it wasn't witchcraft, it was this letter, read it."

And taking a letter from her reticule, she gave it to Barnabas, and watched him while he read:

To Her Grace the Duchess of Camber-hurst
Madam,

In justice to yourself I take occasion to warn Your Grace against the person calling himself Barnabas Beverley. He is, in reality, an impudent imposter of humble birth and mean extraction. His real name and condition I will prove absolutely to Your Grace at another time.

Your Grace's most humble obedt.
Wilfred Chichester

"So you see I'm not a witch, Sir . . . oh no, I'm only an old woman with, among many other useful gifts, a very sharp eye for faces, a remarkable genius for asking questions, and the feminine capacity for adding two and two together, and making them eight.

"So, upon reading this letter, I made enquiries on my own account, with the result that yesterday I drove over to a certain Inn called the Coursing House, and talked with your father. Very handsome he is too, as he always was . . . and I saw him in the heyday of his fame, remember.

"Well, I sipped his ale, very good ale I found it, and while I sipped, we talked. He is very proud of his son, it seems. Joan Beverley was to have married an ugly old wretch of a Marquis, and John Barty is handsome still. But an Inn-keeper, hum!"

"So—that was why my mother ran away, Madam?"

"And Wilfred Chichester knows of this, and will tell Cleone, of course!"

"I think not, at least not yet. You see, he is using this knowledge as a weapon against me."

"Why?"

"I promised to help Ronald Barrymaine. . . ."

"That wretched boy! Well?"

Barnabas told her the whole story.

"You actually threatened Wilfred Chichester with this, and forgot that in finding you to be your mother's son he would prove you to be your father's also?"

"Yes, I—I only remembered my promise."

"But . . . can't you see, if you force him to expose you, it will mean your Social ruin?"

"But then, I gave Her my promise."

"Oh, Barnabas. And now you are still determined to confess your father to Cleone, I suppose?"

"Yes; I dare not speak to her otherwise. How could I, knowing myself an . . ."

"Impudent imposter, Sir? You are so abominably high-minded and heroic. Barnabas . . . it's quite depressing! Ah! There she is on the terrace with the Captain, and I'm sure she has seen you, Barnabas, because she's so vastly unconscious."

And Cleone? With what gracious ease she greeted him. With what clear eyes she looked at him! With what demure dignity she gave him her white hand to kiss!

"Clo dear," said the Duchess, "they're going to talk horses and racing, I know they are—your arm, my love. Now, lead on, gentlemen.

"And now, my dear," she continued, speaking in Cleone's ear, "he simply adores you!"

"Really, Godmother . . . how clever of you!"

said Cleone, her eyes brimful of merriment. "How wonderful you are!"

"Yes, he worships you, and consequently is deceiving you with every breath he draws!"

"Deceiving me. . . !"

"Cleone, he is not what he seems. His very name is false!"

"What do you mean? Ah, no, no . . . I'm sure he would not, and yet . . . oh, Godmother . . . why?"

"Because . . . hush . . . Cleone, he's immensely rich, one of the wealthiest young men in London, and . . . hush! . . . he would be loved for himself alone. So, Cleone, listen, he may perhaps come to you with a wonderful story of poverty and humble birth.

"He may tell you his father was only a . . . a farmer, or a tinker, or a . . . an Inn-keeper. Oh, dear me . . . so delightfully romantic! Therefore, loving him as you do . . ."

"I don't!"

"You may let your heart answer as it would, because with all his wealth, he has a father who . . . hush . . . at one time was the greatest man in all England . . . a powerful man, Clo . . . a famous man, indeed a man of the most striking capabilities."

Later that evening Barnabas and Cleone were walking in the garden.

"Cleone, has love come to you—at last? Tell me!"

My lady walked on for a distance, with head again averted, and with never a word.

"Speak!" said Barnabas, and caught her

hand (unresisting now) and held it to his lips. "Oh, Cleone—answer me!"

Just where they stood, a path led down to the shimmering waters, a narrow and very steep path screened by bending willows. Barnabas descended this path, and turning, reached up his hands to Cleone.

"Come!" he said.

And thus, for a moment, while he looked up into her eyes, she looked down into his, and sighed, and moved towards him, and set her foot upon a pebble.

The next moment Cleone was lying in his arms, and for neither of them was life or the world ever to be the same.

The waning moon was bright enough to show the look in her eyes and the quiver of her mouth as Barnabas stooped above her.

"Cleone! Cleone, can you—do you love me? Oh, my white lady—my woman that I love—do you love me?"

She did not speak, but her eyes answered him, and in that moment Barnabas stooped and kissed her, and held her close and closer, until she sighed and stirred in his embrace.

Then all at once he groaned and set her down, and stood before her with bent head.

"My dear," said he, "oh, my dear!"

"Barnabas?"

"Forgive me, I should have spoken—indeed, I meant to—but I couldn't think, it was so sudden! Forgive me! I didn't mean to even touch your hand until I had confessed my deceit.

"Oh, my dear, I am not—not the fine gentleman you think me. I am only a very humble fellow. The son of a village Inn-keeper. Your eyes were kind to me just now, but oh, Cleone, if so humble a fellow is unworthy, as I fear, I—I will try to forget."

Very still she stood, looking upon his bent head, and she saw that quiver of his lips, and felt the gripping of his strong hands.

Now, when she spoke, her voice was very tender.

"Can you . . . ever forget?"

"I will try!"

"Then, Barnabas, don't. Because I think I could love this humble fellow Barnabas."

Chapter
Seven

But the charm of this pastoral interlude was fleeting, and the very next day found Barnabas back in London, his spirits refreshed and his heart lighter.

Walking in Holborn later in the day, Barnabas espied a face amidst the hurrying throng; a face whose proud, dark beauty there was no mistaking, despite its added look of sorrow; and a figure whose ripe loveliness the threadbare cloak could not disguise.

For a moment her eyes looked up into his, dark and suddenly wide, then, quick and light of foot, she was gone, lost in the bustling crowd.

But even so, Barnabas turned and followed, striding on and on until at length he saw again the flutter of the threadbare cloak.

On she led him, until they came to a shabby dwelling in a grimy street, and there she turned to face him.

Barnabas saw that, with her apron and mobcap, the country serving-maid had vanished quite.

In her stead was a noble woman, proud and stately, whose clear, sad eyes returned his gaze with a gentle dignity.

Clemency indeed was gone, but Beatrix had come to life.

Yet, when Barnabas spoke, he used the name by which he had first known her.

"Clemency," said he, "your father is seeking for you."

"My father! You know him?"

"Yes. I met him—not long ago. His name is Ralph Darville, he told me, and he goes up and down the countryside searching for you—has done so ever since he lost you."

"My father!" she whispered again, with quivering lips. "Preaching?"

"He tramps the roads hoping to find you, Clemency, and he preaches at country wakes and fairs because, he told me, he was once a very selfish man, and unforgiving."

"And . . . oh, you have seen him, you say . . . lately?" she said.

"Yes. And I sent him to Frittenden, to the Spotted Cow. But, Clemency, he was just a day too late."

"Oh, Father! If only I had known, if I could but have guessed! Oh, Father! Father!"

"Clemency, why did you run away?"

"Because I . . . I was afraid!"

"Of Chichester?"

"No. Him I only . . . hate!"

"Then whom did you fear? Was it—the Viscount?"

"No . . . no, I . . . I think it was . . . myself.

172

Oh, I . . . I am very wretched and . . . lonely!" She sobbed. "I want . . . my father!"

"And he shall be found," said Barnabas, "I promise you! But, until then, will you trust me, Clemency, as—as a sister might trust her brother?

"Will you let me take you from this dreary place—will you, Clemency? I—I'll buy you a house—I mean a—a cottage in the country—or anywhere you wish."

"Oh, Mr. Beverley!" She sighed, looking up at him with tear-dimmed eyes, but with the ghost of a smile hovering round her scarlet lips. "I thank you . . . indeed, indeed I do, but how can I? How may I?"

"Quite easily," said Barnabas stoutly, "oh quite—until I bring your father to you."

"Dear, dear Father!" she said, and sighed. "Is he much changed? I wonder. Is he well . . . quite well?"

"Yes, he is very well," answered Barnabas, "but you—indeed, you cannot stay here. . . ."

"I must," she answered. "I can earn enough for my needs with my needle."

"But how did you find your way to such a place as this?"

"Milo brought me here."

"The Viscount's little imp of a groom?"

"Yes, though he promised never to tell *him* where I was, and Milo always keeps his word. And you, Mr. Beverley, you will promise also, won't you?"

"You mean never to tell the Viscount of your whereabouts?"

Clemency nodded.

"Yes," said Barnabas, "I will promise, but—
on condition that you henceforth will regard me as
a brother. That you will allow me the privilege of
helping you whenever I may, and will always turn
to me in your need. Will you promise me this,
Clemency?"

Barnabas held out his hand.

"Yes," she answered, smiling up into his earnest eyes, "I think I shall be proud to have you
for a brother."

And she put her hand into his.

Then she said:

"Mr. Beverley, I want to ask you something
else ... about my father. ... Does he think I am
... does he know that ... though I ran away with
... a beast, I ... ran away ... from him, also
... does he know ... ?"

"He knows you for the sweet, pure woman
you are. He knows the truth, and lives but to find
you again, my sister!"

Now when he said this, Barnabas saw within
her tearful eyes the light of a joy unutterable; so
he bared his head and, turning about, strode
quickly away up the alley.

*   *   *

It was some days after this that the Viscount
burst unannounced into Barnabas's drawing-room
one morning.

Pale, haggard of eye, and dusty and unkempt,
he leaned there, then staggering to a chair he sank
down and so lay staring at the floor.

"Oh, Bev!" he said, and groaned. "She's gone
—Clemency's gone. I—I can't find her, Bev!"

174

"Dick!" cried Barnabas, bending over him. "My dear fellow!"

"I drove down to Frittenden, and oh, Bev, she was gone! So I started back, looking for her all night. But I kept fancying I saw her before me in the dark. Sometimes I called to her, but she never answered. She's gone, Bev, and I . . ."

"Oh, Dick, she left weeks ago. . . ."

"What—you knew? Then oh, Bev—tell me where!"

"Dick, I can't!"

"Why—why?"

"I promised her to keep it secret."

"Then—then you won't tell me? By God, but you shall, I say you shall—you must—she's mine! Mine, I tell you—no one shall take her from me, neither you nor the devil himself.

"Tell me where she is—speak before I choke you—speak!"

But Barnabas stood rigid and utterly still.

Then the Viscount stood up, stepped back, and, groaning, bowed his head.

"Oh, Bev, forgive me, I—I'm mad, I think. I want her so, and I can't find her. Will you tell me where she is?"

"No, but . . ."

"Then, Sir, my further movements need not concern you."

"Dick, if you'll only wait, I'll go to her now —this moment—I'll beg her to see you. . . ."

"Very kind, Sir! You are privileged, it seems. But, by God, I don't need you or anyone else to act as go-between or to plead my cause.

"And mark me, Sir! I'll find her yet. I swear to you, I'll never rest until I find her again.

"And now, Sir, once and for all, I have the honour to wish you a very good day!"

Saying which, the Viscount bowed and walked away down the corridor.

As the Viscount left, Barnabas's footman entered with a letter that took all other thoughts from his head.

Hastily Barnabas broke the seal and read:

> *Oh, Barnabas, dear, when shall I see you again?*
>
> *You ask me if I love you; can you doubt? How often in my dreams have I seen you kneeling beside me with your neck all bare and the dripping kerchief in your hand. Oh, dear Wood of Annersley, it was there that I first felt your arms about me, Barnabas, and I dream of that too... sometimes.*
>
> *Oh, Barnabas, come to me! I want you here beside me, for although the sky here is blue and cloudless, away to the north where London lies, there is a great, black shadow; and God keep all shadows from you, Barnabas. So come to me ... meet me tomorrow, there is a new moon.*
>
> *Come to Oakshott's Barn at 7:30 and we will walk back to the house together.*
>
> *I am longing to see you, and yet I am a little afraid also, because my love is not a quiet love or gentle, but such a love as frightens me sometimes, because it has grown so deep and strong.*
>
> *Your*
> *CLEONE*

176

Now when he had finished reading, Barnabas sighed and sat for a moment staring into space. Then he noticed something that had escaped him at first. The letter had been torn open and sealed again before he had opened it himself.

This for some reason aroused a suspicion in Barnabas's mind, and, on examining the letter more closely, he saw that the paper round the symbols "7:30" was roughened, as if something had been scratched out and those figures written in.

Suppose, thought Barnabas, the letter had been intercepted and tampered with? Oakshott's Barn was a lonely place indeed, and the suspicion in his mind hardened. If he was to be there at 7:30, he knew that it would not be Cleone whom he would meet.

*　　*　　*

Even on a summer's afternoon, Oakshott's Barn is a desolate place, a place of shadows and solitude.

Yet, standing there, Barnabas smiled and uncovered his head, for there, once, She had stood, she who was for him the only woman in all the world.

So, having paused awhile to look about him, he presently went on into the gloom of the barn, a gloom damp and musty with years and decay.

In a while, as he watched, screening himself from all chance of observation, Barnabas saw two figures emerge into the clearing and advance towards the barn.

"I tell you, Ch-Chichester, it will either be him or m-me!"

"But you can't make a man fight, Ronald."

"Can't I? Why then, if he won't fight I'll . . ."

"You don't mean murder, Ronald?"

"I d-didn't s-say so, d-did I?"

"Then, if he refuses to fight you, as of course he will, you'll let him go to—ah—make love to Cleone?"

"No, by God!" cried Barrymaine in a sudden, wild fury. "I—I'll sh-shoot him first!"

"Kill him?"

"Damn him! Damn him! B-bury me in a debtors' prison, will he? Foul my sister's honour, w-will he? Never! Never! I tell you I'll kill him first!"

"Well, the time is getting on, Ronald—nearly seven o'clock, and your ardent lovers are usually before their time. Come into the barn."

"N-no—that devilish dark hole!"

"All the better, Ronald—think of his surprise when instead of finding an armful of warm loveliness waiting for him in the shadows he finds the avenging brother! Come into the shadows, Ronald."

"Yes. Is your f-flask empty, Chichester?"

"Surely you've had enough, Ronald?"

"I'm n-not drunk, I t-tell you. I know when I've had enough. G-give me some brandy, Chit."

"Why then, fix this flint first, Ronald; I see you have all the necessary tools here."

So saying, Mr. Chichester rose and began feeling through his pockets, while Barrymaine, grumbling, stooped above the pistol-case.

Mr. Chichester drew out a silver flask, unscrewed it, and thereafter made a certain quick, stealthy gesture behind his companion's back; which done, he screwed up the flask again, shook it, and, as Barrymaine rose, he held it out to him.

With a murmur of thanks, Barrymaine took the flask and, setting it to his lips, drained it at a gulp, then handed it back.

"Gad, Chichester, it tastes damnably queer. What time is it? I think I'll s-sit down. I'm not—n-not drunk, only dev'lish sleepy!" And, swaying to the wall, he leaned there, with head drooping.

"Then you'd better lie down, Ronald."

"Yes, I'll lie down—dev'lish drowsy p-place—lie down."

Barrymaine sank down upon his side, rolled over onto his back, threw wide his arms, and so lay, breathing stertorously.

Then Mr. Chichester smiled and, going beside him, looked down upon his helpless form.

"Oh, Ronald," he murmured, "what a fool you are, what a drunken, sottish fool you are. So you'd give him a chance, would you? Ah, but you mustn't, Ronald, you shan't, for your sake and my sake.

"My hand is steadier than yours, so sleep, my dear Ronald, and wake to find that you have rid us of our young Good Samaritan once and for all, and then—hey for Cleone, and no more dread of the future. Sleep on, you swinish sot!"

And now Mr. Chichester stooped, and taking the pistols, he crossed to a darkened window, burst open the rotting shutter, knelt, and levelled one of the weapons, steadying his wrist upon the sill.

Then, nodding as though satisfied, he laid the pistols upon the floor within easy reach, and drew out his watch.

Slowly the sun declined, and slowly the shadows lengthened about Oakshott's Barn.

And ever that crouching figure knelt beside the broken shutter, very silent, very still, and very patient.

But all at once, as he watched, Barnabas saw the rigid figure grow suddenly alert, saw the right arm raised slowly, stealthily, saw the pistol gleam as it was levelled across the sill; for now, upon the quiet, rose a sound, faint and far, yet that grew and ever grew, the oncoming rustle of leaves.

Then, even as Barnabas stared down wide-eyed, the rigid figure started, the deadly pistol-hand wavered, was snatched back, and Mr. Chichester leapt to his feet.

He stood for a moment hesitating, as one at a sudden loss; then, crossing to the unconscious form of Barrymaine, he set the pistol under his lax hand, turned, and vanished into the shadows.

But for all the rustling of leaves, no figure appeared, and after a few moments Barnabas emerged from his hiding-place and stepped outside the barn.

Stealthily he walked in among the trees and went about for some minutes without seeing or hearing a thing, before retracing his steps and going back into the barn.

He started back before the threatening figure that rose up from the shadows.

"Ah! So you've c-come at last, Sir!" said Barrymaine, steadying himself against the wall with one hand while he held the pistol levelled in the other. "In-instead of the weak s-sister you find the avenging brother! Been waiting for you hours. C-cursed dreary hole this, and I fell asleep, but . . ."

"Because you were drugged!"

"D-drugged, Sir! W-what d' you mean?"

"Chichester drugged the brandy. . . ."

"Chichester. . . ?"

"He meant to murder me while you slept and fix the crime on you. . . ."

"Liar! You came here to meet my s-sister, but instead of a defenceless girl you meet me, and I'm g-going to settle with you—once and for all—t-told you I would, last time we met. Pick up that pistol—or I'll sh-shoot you where you stand!"

But on the instant Barnabas sprang in and closed with him, and grappled in a fierce embrace; they swayed for a moment and then staggered out through the gaping doorway.

Barrymaine fought desperately, yet twice the muzzle of the weapon covered Barnabas, and twice he eluded it before Barrymaine could fire.

Then Barnabas loosed one hand, drew back his arm, and smote—swift and hard. Barrymaine uttered a cry that seemed to Barnabas to find an echo far off, then he flung out his arms and, staggering, fell.

Ronald Barrymaine lay very white and still, and Barnabas, stooping, saw that he had struck much harder than he had meant, and that Barrymaine's mouth was cut and bleeding.

Now at this moment, even as he sank on his

knees, Barnabas again heard a cry, but nearer now and with the rustle of flying draperies, and glancing up he saw Cleone running towards them.

"You ... struck him!" she said, panting.

"I—yes, I—had to! But, indeed, he isn't much hurt. . . ."

But Cleone was down upon her knees, had lifted Barrymaine's head to her bosom, and with her handkerchief was wiping the blood from his pale face.

"Cleone, I couldn't help it. Oh, Cleone— look up!"

Yet, while he spoke, there came a rustling of leaves nearby, and, glancing thither, he saw Mr. Chichester surveying them, smiling and debonair.

"Ah!" Mr. Chichester nodded gently. "You have a pistol there, I see!"

"Your despicable villainy is known!" said Barnabas. "Ha! Smile if you will, but while you knelt, pistol in hand, in the barn there, had you troubled to look in the loft above your head you might have murdered me, and none the wiser.

"As it is, I am alive, to strip you of your heritage. I swear you shall be hounded from every Club in London, and men shall know you for what you are. Now, go, before you tempt me to strangle you. Go I say!"

Mr. Chichester slowly viewed Barnabas from head to foot; then, turning, he strolled away, swinging his tasselled walking-cane as he went, with Barnabas close behind him, pistol in hand, even as they had once walked months before.

Now at this moment, Cleone, yet kneeling beside Barrymaine, saw a crumpled piece of paper

182

that lay within a yard of her. She reached out and
took it up, glanced at it with vague eyes, then
started, and, knitting her black brows, read these
words:

> My Dear Barnabas,
>   The beast has discovered me. I thought
> I only scorned him, but now I know I fear
> him, too. So, in my dread, I turn to you. Yes,
> I will go now . . . anywhere you wish. Fear
> has made me humble and I accept your offer.
>   Oh, take me away . . . hide me, any-
> where, so shall I always be
>   Your grateful,
>   Clemency

When Barrymaine opened his eyes, it was to
see Cleone kneeling beside him, with bent head,
and with both hands clasped down upon her bosom, fierce hands that clenched between them a
crumpled paper.

At first he thought she was weeping, but when
she turned towards him he saw that her eyes were
tearless and very bright, and that on either cheek
burned a vivid patch of colour.

"Oh, Ronald. I am glad you are better . . . but
. . . oh, my dear, I wish I . . . were dead!"

"There, there, Clo! But I'm all right now,
dear. W-where's Chichester?"

"I . . . don't know, Ronald."

"But you, Cleone? You came here to m-meet
this—this Beverley? D' you know w-what he is?
D' you know he's a Publican's son? A vile, low
fellow masquerading as a g-gentleman.

"And you stoop to such as he—s-stoop to

183

meet him in s-such a place as this! So I came to save you f-from yourself!"

"Did you, Ronald?"

"Yes—but oh, Cleone, you don't l-love this fellow, do you?"

"I think I hate him, Ronald."

"Then you won't m-meet him again?"

"No, Ronald."

"And you'll try to be a little kinder to Ch-Chichester?"

Cleone shivered and rose to her feet.

But as they turned to go, the bushes parted and Barnabas appeared.

"Cleone!".

"I . . . I'm going home!"

"Then I will come with you, if I may?"

"I would rather go alone, with my brother."

"May I come with you, Cleone?"

"No, Sir, n-not while I'm here. Cleone, you go with him or m-me, so choose!"

"Oh, Ronald, take me home!"

So Barrymaine drew her arm through his, and, turning his back on Barnabas, led her away. But when they had gone a little distance, Barnabas frowned suddenly and came striding after them.

"Cleone," said he, "why are you so strange to me? What is it? Speak to me."

But Cleone was dumb, and walked on beside Ronald Barrymaine with head averted, and so, with never a backwards glance, she was presently lost to sight among the leaves.

Long after they had gone, Barnabas stood there, his head bowed, while the shadows deepened about him, darker and darker. Then all at once he uttered a bitter curse and strode away through the deepening gloom.

As for my lady, securely locked within the sanctuary of her chamber, she took pen and paper and wrote these words:

You have destroyed my faith, and with that all else.

Farewell.

Which done, she stamped a small yet vicious foot upon a certain crumpled letter, and thereafter, lying face down upon her bed, wept hot, slow, bitter tears, stifling her sobs with the tumbled glory of her hair.

In her heart was an agony greater than any she had ever known before.

* * *

In response to Clemency's letter, which, all unbeknownst, had been the cause of Barnabas's misery, he went the next day to her poor lodgings in Blackfriars, intending, as he had promised, to take her away with him.

Coming to her door, he knocked with his cane. It was opened almost immediately, by Clemency herself.

"I came as soon as I could, Clemency. I am here to take you away to a cottage I have found for you—a place in the country, where you will be safe until I can find and bring your father to you."

As he ended, she lifted her head and looked at him through gathering tears.

"But I must stay here."

"In this awful place? Why?"

"Because *he* is so ill ... dangerously ill, Milo tells me, and I ... I am nearer to him here in London. I can go, sometimes, and look at the house where he lies. So, you see, I cannot leave him yet."

"Then you love him, Clemency?"

"Yes," she whispered, "yes, oh yes, always ... always! That was why I ran away from him. Oh, I love him so much that I grew afraid of my love, and of myself, and of him. Because he is a great gentleman, and I am only ... what I am."

"A very good and beautiful woman?"

"Beauty! Oh, it is only for that he wanted me, and dear heaven!—I love him so much that if he asked me ... I fear ..."

She hid her burning face in hands that trembled.

"Clemency!"

The word was scarcely more than a whisper, but Clemency started and lifted her head to stare wide-eyed at the figure leaning in the doorway, with one hand outstretched to her appealingly.

A tall figure, cloaked from head to foot, with hat drawn low over his brows, his right arm carried in a sling.

"My Lord! Oh, My Lord!"

"Dearest!"

The Viscount stepped into the room and, uncovering his head, sank upon his knees before her.

"Oh, Clemency, the door was open and I heard it all—every word. But, dearest, you need never fear me any more—never any more, because

I love you, Clemency, and here, upon my knees, I beg you to honour me by marrying me, if you will stoop to such a pitiful thing as I am.

"Clemency, dear, I have been ill, and it has taught me many things, and I know now that I cannot live without you. So, Clemency, if you will take pity on me—oh, Clemency . . ."

The Viscount stopped, still kneeling before her with bent head, nor did he look up, nor attempt to touch her, as he awaited her answer.

Then, slowly, she sank to her knees before him, so that now he could look into the glowing beauty of her face and behold the deep, yearning tenderness in her eyes.

"Dear, if you want me so much, you have only to . . . take me!"

"For my Viscountess, Clemency!"

"For your wife, dear!"

Beholding their great happiness, Barnabas stole from the room, closing the door softly behind him, and, being only human, he sighed deeply and pitied himself mightily by contrast, as he went on his way.

Passing along a dark street by the river, he heard a familiar voice.

"Oh, Lord God of the weary and heavy-hearted, have mercy upon me! Oh, Father of the Sorrowful, suffer now that I find rest!"

The Apostle of Peace stood before him, his silver hair shining, his pale face uplifted towards heaven.

"You are alive, young Sir, which is good, and your hands are not stained with a villain's

187

blood, which is much better. But, as for me—God pity me—I came here tonight meaning to be a self-murderer—oh, God forgive me!"

"But you asked for—a sign, I think," said Barnabas, "and you live also. And tonight your pilgrimage ends, in Clemency's loving arms."

"Clemency? My daughter? Sir, young sir, how may that be? They tell me she is dead."

"Lies!" said Barnabas. "Lies! I spoke with her tonight."

The Apostle of Peace stood awhile with bowed head; when at last he looked up, his cheeks were wet with tears.

"Then, Sir, take me to her!"

So, without more ado, they left that dreary place, and walked on together, side by side and very silent, Barnabas with drooping head, and his companion with eyes uplifted and ever-moving lips.

They turned into the narrow court, Barnabas knocked, and, as they waited, he could see that his companion was trembling violently where he leaned beside him against the wall.

Then the door was opened and Clemency appeared.

"Mr. Beverley, dear brother, is it you?"

"Yes, Clemency, and—and I have kept my promise, I have brought you . . ."

But no need for words; Clemency had seen.

"Father!" she cried, stretching out her arms. "Oh, dear Father!"

"Beatrix, oh, my child—forgive me . . ."

But Clemency had caught him in her arms, and pillowing the silvery head upon her young bosom, she folded it there, and so hung above him all sighs and tears and tender endearments.

Then Barnabas closed the door upon them, and sighing went on his way, conscious only of the dull ache at his heart, and the ever-growing doubt and fear within him.

Chapter
Eight

The star of Barnabas Beverley, Esquire, was undoubtedly in the ascendent.

For here was one, not only young, fabulously rich, and a proved sportsman, but a Dandy besides, with a nice taste and originality in waistcoats and cravats, which as the Fashionable World well knows are the final gauge of a man's depth and possibilities.

Nevertheless, Barnabas Beverley was not happy, for though his smile was as ready as his tongue, his brow would at times grow dark and sombre. Yet even this was accepted in all good faith, and consequently pale cheeks and a romantic gloom became the mode.

No, indeed, Barnabas was not happy, since he must think ever of Cleone. Two letters had he written her, the first a humble supplication, the second an angry demand couched in terms of bitter reproach.

Yet Cleone gave no sign; and the days passed.

Therefore, being himself young and proud, he wrote no more, and waited for some word of explanation, some sign from her; then, as the days lengthened into weeks, he set himself resolutely to forget her, if such a thing might be.

The better to achieve a thing so impossible, he turned to that most fickle of all goddesses, whose name is Chance.

He became a familiar figure at those very select gaming-tables where play was highest, and tales of his recklessness began to circulate.

Thus a fortnight had elapsed, and tonight the star of Barnabas Beverley, Esquire, has indeed attained its grand climacteric, for tonight he is to eat and drink with *Royalty,* and the Fashionable World is to do him honour.

Never had White's, that historic Club, gathered beneath its roof a more distinguished company; Dukes, Royal and otherwise, elbow one another on the stairs; Earls and Marquises sit cheek by jowl; Viscounts and Baronets exchange snuffboxes in the corners.

Yes, White's is full to overflowing, for tonight half the Fashionable World is here—that is to say, the masculine half; Beaux and wits; Bucks and Corinthians; all are here, each and every one, with the fixed and unshakable purpose of eating and drinking to the glory and honour of Barnabas Beverley, Esquire.

Forthwith the Banquet begins and the air hums with talk and laughter, punctuated by the popping of corks; waiters hurry to and fro, dishes come and dishes vanish, and ever the laughter grows, and the buzz of talk swells louder.

Thus Barnabas sits among the glare and glitter of it all, smiling at one, bowing to another, speaking with all by turns, and wondering in his heart if there is yet any letter from Hawkhurst.

And now, in their turn, diverse, noble gentlemen rise in their places and deliver speeches, more or less eloquent, flowery, witty, and laudatory; but, one and all, full of the name and the excellencies of Barnabas Beverley, Esquire.

To all of which he listens with varying emotions, and with one eye upon the door, fervently hoping for the letter so long expected.

But the time is come for him to respond; all eyes are upon him, and all glasses are filled; even the waiters become deferentially interested, as, amidst welcoming shouts, the guest of the evening rises, a little flushed, a little nervous, yet steady of eye.

As Barnabas stands there, an elegant figure, tall and graceful, all eyes may behold again the excellent fit of that wonderful coat, while all ears await his words.

But before even he can speak, upon this silence is heard the tread of heavy feet beyond the door, and Barnabas glances thither eagerly, ever mindful of the letter from Hawkhurst.

But the feet have stopped, and stifling a sigh, he begins:

"My Lords and gentlemen! So much am I conscious of the profound honour you do me that I find it difficult to express my . . ."

But here again a disturbance is heard at the door, a shuffle of feet and the mutter of voices, and he pauses, expectant; whereat his auditors cry angrily for "Silence!" which, being duly accorded, he begins again:

"Indeed, gentlemen, I fear no words of mine, however eloquent, can sufficiently express to you all my . . ."

"Oh, Barnabas," cries a deep voice; "yes, it is Barnabas!"

Even as the words are uttered, the group of protesting waiters in the doorway are swept aside by a mighty arm, and a figure strides into the banqueting-room, a handsome figure, despite its country habiliments, a commanding figure by reason of its stature and great spread of shoulder.

John Barty stands there, blinking in the light of the many candles.

Then Barnabas closed his eyes and, reaching out, set his hand upon the back of a chair nearby, and so stood with bent head and a strange roaring in his ears.

Little by little this noise grew less until he could hear voices about him, an angry clamour:

"Put him out!"

"Throw the rascal into the street!"

"Kick him downstairs, somebody!"

And, amidst this ever-growing tumult, Barnabas could distinguish his father's voice, and in it was a note he had never heard before, something of pleading, something of fear.

"Barnabas? Barnabas? Oh, this be you, my lad—bean't it, Barnabas?"

Yet still he stood with bent head, his fingers clenched hard upon the chair-back, while the clamour about him grew ever louder and more threatening.

"Jove!" exclaimed the Marquis, rising and buttoning his coat. "If nobody else will, I'll have a try at him myself. Come now, my good fellow, you must either get out of here or—put 'em up, you know."

But as he advanced, Barnabas lifted his head, and, staying him with a gesture, turned and beheld his father standing alone, at the centre of an angry circle.

John Barty's eyes were wide and troubled, and his usually ruddy cheeks showed pale, though with something more than fear, as, glancing slowly round the ring of the threatening figures that hemmed him in, he beheld the white, stricken face of his son.

And seeing it, John Barty groaned, and so took a step towards the door.

"A—a mistake, gentlemen," he muttered. "I—I'll go!"

Then, even as the stammering words were uttered, Barnabas strode forward into the circle, and, slipping a hand within his father's arm, looked round upon the company, pale of cheek but with head carried high.

"My Lords! Gentlemen! I have the honour to introduce to you—John Barty, sometimes known as 'Glorious John'—ex-Champion of England, and —Landlord of the Coursing Hound Inn—my father!"

A moment of silence! A long, long moment wherein Barnabas felt himself a target for all eyes —eyes wherein he saw amazement that changed into dismay, which in turn gave place to an ever-growing scorn of him.

Therefore, he turned his back upon them all, and stood staring blindly into the dark street.

"Oh, Barnabas!" he heard his father saying, though as from a long way off. "Barnabas, lad, they're going! They're leaving you, and it's all my fault, lad! Oh, Barnabas—what have I done!

"But I heard you were sick, Barnabas, and like to die—ill and calling for me—for your father, Barnabas. And now, my lad! what have I done?"

"Never blame yourself, Father, it—wasn't your fault," said Barnabas with twitching lips.

From the great room behind him came the clatter of chairs and the tread of feet, with voices and stifled laughter that grew fainter and fainter, yet left a sting behind.

Now in a while Barnabas turned back; the banqueting-hall was empty, that is to say—very nearly.

Of all that brilliant and fashionable company but two remained: the Viscount, crumbling up bread and staring at the table-cloth, and the Marquis, fidgeting with his snuff-box, and frowning at the ceiling.

"Sirs," said Barnabas, "I think you'd better go. You will be less—conspicuous. Indeed, you'd better go."

"Go?" repeated the Viscount, rising suddenly. "Go, is it? No, damme if we do! If you are John Barty's son, you are still my friend, and—there's my hand—Barnabas."

"Mine—too!" The Marquis sneezed. "S-soon as I've got over the 'ffects of this s-snuff—with a curse to it!"

"Sir," said Barnabas, reaching out and grasping a hand of each, "with your friendship to hearten me—all things are possible—even this!"

But here a waiter appeared, bearing a tray, and on the tray was a letter. Barnabas took it and, breaking the seal, read these words in Cleone's writing:

You have destroyed my faith, and with that all else.

Farewell.

Then Barnabas laughed, sudden and sharp, and tore the paper across and across, and, dropping the pieces to the floor, set his foot upon them.

"Friends," said he, "my future is decided for me.

"Tonight I leave the World of Fashion for one better suited to my birth, for it seems I should be only an Amateur Gentleman, as it were, after all. My Lords, your most obedient, humble servant—good-bye!"

So Barnabas bowed to each in turn, and went forth from the scene of his triumph, deliberate of step and with head carried high, as became a conqueror.

Thus the star of Barnabas Beverley, Esquire, waxed, waned, and vanished utterly from the Fashionable Firmament, and in time came to be regarded as only a comet, after all.

*   *   *

Barnabas walked the streets for an hour or more, neither knowing nor caring where he went.

At last, tired and miserable, he stopped out-

197

side a house that seemed familiar to him. With a start he recognised the home of Jasper Gaunt, and in that same moment he felt an overwhelming compulsion to enter.

Going to the door, Barnabas lifted his hand to knock, yet stood again, hesitating. Then, quickly and suddenly, he threw wide the door and stepped into the room.

A candle flared and by this flickering light he saw an overturned chair, a litter of scattered papers and documents, and beyond that, Jasper Gaunt seated at his desk in the corner. He was lolling back in his chair like one asleep; and yet—was this sleep?

Something in the appalling stillness of that lolling figure filled Barnabas with a nameless, growing horror. He took a step nearer, another, and another, then stopped, and, uttering a choking gasp, fell back to the wall and leaned there, suddenly faint and sick.

For, indeed, this was more than sleep. Jasper Gaunt lolled there with his head at a hideous angle, and the dagger—which had been wont to glitter so evilly from the wall—smitten sideways through his throat.

Barnabas crouched against the wall, and as he closed his eyes the faintness grew upon him. At length he sighed and moved a backwards step toward the door; thus it was that he chanced to see Jasper Gaunt's right hand.

And in that rigid grasp was something that struck Barnabas to action. He forced open those stiffening fingers and drew from their dead clutch something that he stared at with white lips suddenly compressed, before he hid it away in his pocket.

Then, shivering, he backed away, feeling behind him for the door, and so went out into the passage and down the stairs, and straight to the house of Ronald Barrymaine.

Passing into the house and up the stairs, Barnabas entered the top room and looked into the haggard face of Ronald Barrymaine.

"Beverley! W-what d' you want? Go away—I-leave me!"

"No!" said Barnabas. "It is you who must go away—at once. You must leave London tonight!"

"W-what d' you mean?"

"You must be clear of England by tomorrow night at the latest."

Barrymaine stared up at Barnabas wide-eyed and passed his tongue to and fro across his lips before he spoke again.

"Beverley, w-what d' you mean?"

"I know why you keep your right hand hidden!"

Barrymaine shivered suddenly, and upon his furrowed brow and pallid cheek ran glittering lines of sweat. At last he contrived to speak again, but in a whisper now:

"W-what do you mean?"

"I mean that tonight I found this scrap of cloth, and I recognised it as part of the cuff of your sleeve, and I found it clenched in Jasper Gaunt's dead hand."

"Oh, Beverley, I s-swear to you I n-never meant to do it. I went there tonight to l-learn the t-truth, and he threatened me, s-so we fought and he was s-strong and swung me against the w-wall. And then, Beverley—as we s-struggled—somehow I g-got hold of—of the dagger, and struck at him —b-blindly.

"And—oh, my God, Beverley—I shall never forget how he ch-choked! I can hear it now! But I didn't mean to do it. Oh, I s-swear I never meant it, Beverley—s-so help me, God!

"I wronged you, I know n-now, but don't g-give me up. I'm not afraid to d-die like a g-gentleman should, but—the gallows—oh, my God!"

"No, you must be saved—from that!"

"Beverley, I wronged you, but I know now who my c-creditor really is—I know who has been m-my enemy all along—oh, blind f-fool that I've been—but I know now."

"Yes, but now, take off that coat."

"But it's the only one I've got!"

"You shall have mine," said Barnabas, and, throwing aside his cloak, he stripped off that marvellous garment and laid it upon the table beside Barrymaine.

"I—oh, I—Beverley, I—c-can't!"

And now, all at once, as they stared into each other's eyes, Barnabas leaning forward, strong and compelling, Barrymaine upon his knees, clinging weakly to the table, sudden and sharp upon the stillness broke a sound, an ominous sound, the stumble of a foot that mounted the stair.

Uttering a broken cry, Barrymaine struggled up to his feet, strove desperately to speak, his distorted mouth flecked with foam, and, beating the air with frantic hands, pitched over and thudded to the floor.

Then the door opened and Mr. Smivvle appeared, who, calling Barrymaine's name, ran forward and fell upon his knees beside that convulsed and twisted figure.

"My God, Beverley!" he cried. "How comes he like this—what has happened?"

"Tonight he killed Jasper Gaunt."

"Killed him? Murdered him?"

"Yes. Pull yourself together and listen. Tomorrow the hue and cry will be all over London, so we must get him away—out of the country if possible."

"Yes, yes—of course! But he's ill—a fit, I think."

"Have you ever seen him so before?"

"Never so bad as this. There, Barry, there, my poor fellow! Help me to get him on the couch, will you, Beverley?"

Between them they raised that twitching form; then, as Mr. Smivvle stooped to set a cushion beneath the restless head, he started suddenly back, staring wide-eyed and pointing with a shaking finger.

"My God!" he whispered. "What's that? Look —look at his coat. See—it's—it's—all down the front!"

"If this coat is ever found, it will hang him! Come, help me to get it off."

So between them it was done, and while Mr. Smivvle crouched beside that restless, muttering form, Barnabas put on his cloak and, rolling up the torn coat, hid it beneath his cloak's ample folds.

"What, are you going, Beverley?"

"Yes—for one thing, to get rid of this coat. On the table are twenty guineas; take them, and just so soon as Barrymaine is fit to travel, get him away.

"If he isn't better by morning, get a Doctor, but whatever you do—keep Chichester away from him. As regards money, I'll see you shan't want for it. And now, for the present, good-bye!"

So saying, Barnabas caught up his hat, and, with a last glance at the moaning figure on the couch, went from the room and down the stairs, and let himself out into the dingy street.

* * *

It was long past midnight when Barnabas reached his house in St. James's Square. Gazing up at its goodly exterior, he sighed, and thereafter frowned, and so, frowning still, let himself in.

Now, late though the hour, Peterby was up, and met him in the hall.

"Sir," he said, anxious of eye as he beheld his young master's disordered dress and the grim pallor of his face, "the Marquis of Jerningham and Viscount Devenham called. They waited for you—they waited over an hour."

"But they are gone now, of course?" enquired Barnabas, pausing with his foot on the stair.

"Yes, Sir . . ."

"Good!" Barnabas nodded with a sigh of relief.

"But they left word they would call tomorrow morning early; indeed, they seemed most anxious to see you, Sir."

"Ha!" said Barnabas, and, frowning still, went up on the stair.

"Sir," said Peterby, lighting the way into the dressing-room, "you received the—the letter safely?"

"Yes, I received it," said Barnabas, tossing aside his hat and cloak. "And that reminds me, tomorrow morning you will discharge all the servants."

"Sir?"

"Pay them a month's wages. Also, you will get rid of this house and furniture, and all the carriages and horses—except The Terror—sell them for what they will fetch—no matter how little—only, get rid of them."

"Yes, Sir."

"As for yourself, Peterby, I shall require your services no longer. But you needn't lack for a position—every dandy of 'em will be wild to get you. And, because you are the very best valet in the world, you can demand your own terms."

"Yes, Sir."

"And now I think that is all; I shan't want you again tonight—stay, though, before I go to bed, and bring me the things I wore when I first met you, the garments which, as clothes, you told me, didn't exist."

"Sir, may I ask you a question?"

"Oh, yes—if you wish," said Barnabas, sighing wearily.

"Are you leaving London, Sir?"

"I'm leaving the World of Fashion—yes."

"And you don't wish me to accompany you, Sir?"

"No."

"Have I—displeased you in any way?"

"No, it is only that the 'best valet in the world' would be wasted on me any longer, and I shall not need you where I am going."

"Not as a servant, Sir?"

"No."

"Then, Sir, may I remind you that I am also a man. A man who owes all that he is to your generosity and noble trust and faith. And, Sir, it seems to me that a man may sometimes venture where a servant may not.

"If you are indeed done with the Fashionable World, I have done with it also, for I shall never serve any other than you."

Then Barnabas turned away, and going to the mantel leaned there, staring blankly down at the empty hearth; and in a while he spoke, though without looking up.

"The Fashionable World has turned its polite back upon me, Peterby, because I am only the son of a village Inn-keeper. But—much more than this —my lady has—has lost her faith in me, my fool's dream is over—nothing matters any more. And so I am going away."

"Sir," said Peterby, "when do we start?"

Then, very slowly, Barnabas lifted his heavy head and looked at John Peterby; and, in that dark hour, he smiled, and, reaching out, caught and grasped his hand; also, when he spoke again, his voice was less hard and not so steady as before.

"Oh, John!" said he, "John Peterby—my faithful John! Come with me if you will, but you come as my friend."

"And—where are we going, Sir?" enquired
John, as they stood thus, hand in hand, looking into each other's eyes.

"Giles's Rents, John—down by the river."

And thus did Barnabas, in getting rid of the
"best valet in the world," find for himself a faithful
friend instead.

* * *

Some days later, Barnabas went back to Barrymaine's lodgings. He took an intricate course by
winding alleys and narrow side-streets, keeping his
glance well about him until at length he came to a
certain door in a certain dingy street.

The faulty latch yielded to his hand, he entered a narrow, dingy hall, and he groped his way
up the dingiest stairs in the world.

Now all at once he fancied he heard a stealthy
footstep that climbed on in the darkness before
him, and he paused suddenly, but then, hearing
nothing, strode on, then stopped again, for, plain
enough this time, someone stumbled on the stair
above him.

So he stood there in the gloom, very still and
very silent, and thus he presently heard another
sound, very soft and faint, like the breathing of a
sigh. And all at once Barnabas clenched his teeth
and spoke.

"Who is it?" he demanded fiercely. "Now, by
God, if it's you, Chichester . . ."

With the word, he reached out before him
in the dark with merciless, gripping hands.

The contact of something warm and soft; a
broken, pitiful cry of fear, and he had a woman in

205

his arms. But, even as he clasped that yielding form, Barnabas knew instinctively who it was, and straightway thrilled with a wild joy.

"Madam!" he said hoarsely. "Madam!"

But she never stirred; nay, it almost seemed she sank yet closer into his embrace, if that could well be.

"Cleone!" he whispered.

"Barnabas!" sighed a voice.

Surely no other voice in all the world could have uttered the name so tenderly.

"I—I fear I frightened you?"

"Yes, a little . . . Barnabas."

"You are trembling very much."

"Am I . . . Barnabas?"

"I am sorry that I frightened you."

"I'm better now."

"Yet you tremble!"

"But I think I can walk, if . . ."

"If . . . ?"

"If you will help me, please . . . Barnabas."

Oh, surely never had those dark and dingy stairs, worn though they were by the treadings of countless feet, heard till now a voice so soft, so low and sweet, so altogether irresistible!

"It's so very dark," she said with a sigh.

"Yes, it's very dark," said Barnabas, "but it isn't far to the landing—shall we go up?"

"Yes, but . . ."

My lady hesitated a moment as one who takes breath for some great effort, and in that moment he felt her bosom heave beneath his hand.

"Oh, Barnabas," she whispered, "won't you . . . kiss me . . . first?"

Then Barnabas trembled, in his turn, the arm about her grew suddenly rigid, and when he spoke his voice was harsh and strained.

"Madam," he said, "can the mere kiss of an Inn-keeper's son restore your dead faith?"

Now when he said this, Cleone shrank in his embrace and uttered a low cry as if he had offered her some great wrong, and, breaking from him, she was gone before him up the stairs, running in the dark.

So Barnabas hurried after her, and thus, as she threw open Barrymaine's door he entered with her, and in his sudden abasement he would have knelt to her, but Ronald Barrymaine had sprung up from the couch and now leaned there, staring with dazed eyes, like one new awakened from sleep.

"Ronald!" she cried, running to him. "I came as soon as I could, but I didn't understand your letter. You wrote of some great danger. Oh, Ronald dear, what is it . . . this time?"

"D-danger!" he repeated, and with the word turned to stare over his shoulder into the dingiest corner. "D-danger, yes, so I am—but t-tell me who it is—behind me, in the corner."

"No one, Ronald."

"Yes—yes, there is, I tell you," he whispered. "Look again—now, d-don't you see him?"

"No, oh no!" answered Cleone, clasping her hands and shrinking before Barrymaine's wild and haggard look. "Oh, Ronald, there's no one there!"

"Yes, there is, he's always there now—always just behind me. L-last night he began to talk to me—ah, no, no—what am I saying?—never heed me, Clo.

"I—I asked you to come because I'm g-going away, soon, very s-soon, Clo, and I know I shall n-never see you again. I suppose you thought it was m-money I wanted, but no—it's not that; I wanted to say good-bye because you see I'm g-going away—tonight!"

"Going away, Ronald?" she repeated, sinking to her knees beside the rickety couch, for he had fallen back there as though overcome by sudden weakness. "Dear boy, where are you going . . . and why?"

"I'm g-going far away—because I must—the s-sooner the better!" he whispered, struggling to his elbow to peer into the corner again. "Yes, the s-sooner the better. But before I go I want you to promise, to swear, Clo—to s-swear to me n-never to see or have anything to do with that d-devil Chichester; d' ye hear me, Clo, d' ye hear me?"

"But . . . oh, Ronald, I don't understand. You always told me he was your friend, and I thought . . ."

"Friend!" cried Barrymaine passionately. "He's a devil, I tell you, he's a d-devil, and, oh . . ."

Barrymaine choked and fell back, gasping.

And, even as Cleone leaned above him, all tender solicitude, Barrymaine pushed her aside, sprang to his feet, reached out and caught Barnabas by the arm.

"Beverley!" he cried. "You'll shield her from him—w-when I'm gone you'll look after her, won't you, Beverley? She's the only one I ever loved—except my accursed self. You will shield her from that d-devil!"

208

Then, still clutching Barnabas, he turned and seized Cleone's hands.

"Clo!" he cried, "dearest of sisters, if ever you need a f-friend when I'm gone, he's here. Turn to him, Clo—look up—give him your hand. Y-you loved him once, I think, and you were right—quite right. You can t-trust Beverley, Clo—g-give him your hand."

"No, no!" cried Cleone, and, snatching her fingers from Barrymaine's clasp, she turned away.

"What—you w-won't?"

"No . . . never, never!"

"Why not? Answer me! Speak, I tell you!"

But Cleone knelt there beside the couch, her head proudly averted, and uttered no word.

"Why, you don't, like so many of the fools, think that he killed Jasper Gaunt, do you?" cried Barrymaine feverishly. "You don't believe all the rumours that he was seen leaving there the night before the body was found?

"You don't think he d-did it, do you—do you?

"Ah, but he didn't—he didn't, I tell you, and I know—because . . ."

"Stop!" exclaimed Barnabas.

"Stop—no, why should I? She'll learn soon enough now, and I'm m-man enough to tell her myself—I'm no c-coward, I tell you. . . ."

Then Cleone raised her head and looked up at her half-brother, and in her eyes was a slow-dawning fear and horror.

"Oh, Ronald!" she whispered. "What do you mean?"

209

"Mean?" cried Barrymaine. "I mean that I did it—I did it! Yes, I k-killed Jasper Gaunt, but it was no m-murder, Clo—a—a fight, an accident —yes! I s-swear to God I never meant to do it."

"You!" she whispered. "You?"

"Yes, I—I did it, but I swear I never m-meant to. . . . Oh, Cleone . . ."

He reached down to her with hands outstretched appealingly.

But Cleone shrank down and down away from him until she was crouching on the floor, staring up at him with wide and awful eyes.

"You!" she whispered.

"Don't!" he cried. "Ah, don't look at me like that! And—oh, my God!—w-won't you l-let me t-touch you, Clo?"

"I . . . I'd rather you . . . wouldn't."

Barnabas saw that she was shivering violently.

"But it was no m-murder," he said, pleadingly, "and I'm g-going away, Clo. Ah! won't you let me k-kiss you good-bye—just once, Clo?"

"I'd rather . . . you wouldn't," she whispered.

"Y-your hand, then—only your hand, Clo."

"I'd rather you didn't!"

Then Ronald Barrymaine groaned and fell to his knees beside her, and sought to kiss her little foot, the hem of her dress, a strand of her long, yellow hair; but, seeing how she shuddered away from him, a great sob broke from him and he rose to his feet.

"Beverley," he said, "oh, Beverley, sh-she won't let me touch her."

After a moment he looked down at her again,

210

but, seeing how she yet gazed at him with that wide, awful, fixed stare, he strove as if to speak.

Finding no words, he turned suddenly upon his heel and, crossing the room, went into his bed-chamber and locked the door.

Then Barnabas knelt beside that shaken, desolate figure and fain would have comforted her, but now he could hear her speaking in a passionate whisper, and the words she uttered were these:

"O God, forgive him! O God help him! Have mercy upon him, O God of Pity!"

And these words she whispered over and over again, until, at length, Barnabas reached out and touched her very gently.

"Cleone!" he said.

At the touch she rose and stood looking round the dingy room like one distraught, and, sighing, crossed unsteadily to the door.

When they reached the stairs, Barnabas would have taken her hand because of the dark, but she shrank away from his and shook her head.

"Sir," she said very softly, "a murderer's sister needs no help, I thank you."

So they went down the dark stairs with never a word between them, and, reaching the front door, which had a faulty latch, Barnabas held it open and they passed out into the dingy street.

As they walked side by side towards Hatton Garden, Barnabas saw that her eyes were still fixed and wide and her lips still moved in silent prayer.

* * *

A bad place by day, an evil place by night, an unsavoury place at all times is Giles's Rents, down by the river.

It is a place of noisome courts and alleys, of narrow, crooked streets, where Vice is rampant and ghoulish Hunger stalks, pale and grim.

Truly an unholy place is Giles's Rents, down by the river.

Here, upon a certain evening, Barnabas, leaning out from his narrow casement, turned, wistful-eyed, to stare away over broken roof and crumbling chimney, away beyond the maze of squalid courts and alleys that hemmed him in.

Across the river, the sun was setting in a blaze of glory, yet a glory that served only to make more apparent all the filth and decay, all the sordid ugliness of his surroundings.

He was roused by the opening of the door, and, glancing up, he beheld John Peterby.

The gentleman's gentleman had vanished quite, and in his stead was a nondescript character such as might have been met with anywhere along by the river, or lounging in shadowy corners.

He carried a bundle beneath one arm, and cast a swift look round the room before turning to close the door behind him.

"Ah," said Barnabas, nodding, "I'm glad you're back, John—and with plenty of provisions, I hope, for I'm amazingly hungry, and besides, I've asked a gentleman to sup with us."

Peterby put down the bundle, and, crossing to the hearth, took the kettle, in which water was boiling furiously, and set it upon the hob. Then, laying aside his fur cap, he said:

"A gentleman, Sir?"

"A neighbour, John."

"Sir," said he, as he began to prepare the tea in that swift, silent manner peculiar to him in all things, "when do you propose we shall leave this place?"

"Why, to tell you the truth, John, I had almost determined to start for the country this very night, but, on second thought, I've decided to stay on awhile. After all, we have been here only a week as yet."

"Yes, Sir, it is just a week since Jasper Gaunt was murdered," said Peterby gently, as he stooped to unpack his bundle.

Now when he said this, Barnabas turned to look at him again, and thus he noticed that Peterby's brow was anxious and care-worn.

"I wish, John," said he, "that you would remember we are no longer master and man."

"Old habits stick, Sir."

"And that I brought you to this dismal place as my friend."

"But surely, Sir, a man's friend is worthy of his trust and confidence?"

"John Peterby, what do you mean?"

"Sir," said Peterby, setting down the tea-pot, "as I came along this evening I met a friend; he recognised me in spite of my disguise, and he told me to warn you that . . ."

"Well, John?"

"That you may be arrested . . ."

213

"Yes, John?"

"For the murder of Jasper Gaunt. Oh, Sir, why have you aroused suspicion against yourself by disappearing at such a time?"

"Suspicion?" said Barnabas, and with the word he rose, laid his hands upon John Peterby's shoulders, and looked into his eyes.

Then, seeing the look they held, Barnabas smiled and shook his head.

"Oh, friend," he said, "what matters it so long as you know my hands are clean?"

"But, Sir, if you are arrested . . ."

"They must next prove me guilty, John," said Barnabas, sitting down at the table.

"Or an accessory-after-the-fact!"

"Hum!" said Barnabas thoughtfully. "I never thought of that."

"And, Sir," continued Peterby, anxiously, "there are two Bow Street Runners lounging outside in the court. . . ."

"But they're not after me yet. So cheer up, John!"

Yet, in that moment, Peterby sprang to his feet, with fists clenched, for someone was knocking softly at the door.

"Quick, Sir—the other room—hide!" he whispered.

But, shaking his head, Barnabas rose and, putting him gently aside, opened the door and beheld a small gentleman, who bowed.

"Gentlemen," said the small man, coughing nervously behind his hand, "hem—I trust I don't intrude. Feel it my obligation to pay my respects

214

to—hem!—to welcome you as a neighbour—as a neighbour. Arthur Bimby, humbly at your service."

"Happy to see you, Sir," answered Barnabas, returning his bow with one as deep. "I am Barnabas Barty, at your service, and this is my friend John Peterby. We are about to have supper—nothing very much—tea, Sir, eggs, and a cold fowl, but if you would honour us . . ."

Then, while Peterby hastened to set the comestibles before him, Barnabas drew up a chair.

With many bows and flutterings of his thin, restless hands, the little gentleman sat down.

"Ah!" said he, when at length his hunger was somewhat assuaged. "You are noticing the patch in my left elbow, Sir?"

"No, indeed!" began Barnabas.

"In me, Sirs, you behold a decayed gentleman, yet one who has lived in his time; but now, Sirs, all that remains to me is this coat. A Prince once commended it, and the Beau himself condescended to notice it.

"Yes, Sirs, I was rich once, and happily married, and my friends were many. But—my best friend deceived and ruined me, my wife fled away and left me, Sirs, my friends all forsook me; and today, all that I have to remind me of what I was when I was young, and lived, is this old coat.

"Today I exist as a law-writer; today I am old, and with my vanished youth hope has vanished too. And I call myself a decayed gentleman because I'm—fading, Sirs.

"But to fade is genteel: Brummell faded! Yes, one may fade and still be a gentleman, but who ever heard of a fading ploughman?"

"Who indeed?" said Barnabas.

"Yet, to fade, Sir," continued the little gentleman, lifting a thin, bloodless hand, "though genteel, is a slow process, and a very weary one. Without the companionship of Hope, life becomes a hard and extreme long road to ultimate end, and therefore I am sometimes greatly tempted to take the easier course, the—shorter way."

"What do you mean?"

"Well, Sir, there are other names for it, but —hem!—I prefer to call it 'the shorter way.' "

"Do you mean—suicide?"

"Sir," cried Mr. Bimby, shivering as he raised protesting hands, "I said 'the shorter way.' Poor little Miss Pell—a lady born, Sir—she used to curtsey to me on the stairs—she chose the 'shorter way.' She also was old, you see, and weary.

"And tonight I met another who sought to take this 'shorter way,' but he was young, and for the young there is always hope. So I brought him home with me and tried to comfort him, but I fear—"

Peterby sprang suddenly to his feet and Mr. Bimby started and turned to glance fearfully towards the door.

* * *

It needed but a glance at the huddled figure in the comfortless little attic to assure Barnabas of the identity of Mr. Bimby's "poor young friend"; wherefore, setting down the candle on the broken table, he crossed the room and touched that desolate figure with a gentle hand.

Then Ronald Barrymaine looked up and, seeing Barnabas, struggled to his knees.

"Beverley!" he exclaimed. "Oh, thank God! You'll save her from that d-devil—I tried to kill him, b-but he was too quick for me. But you—you'll save her!"

"What do you mean? Is it Cleone? What do you mean? Speak!" said Barnabas, beginning to tremble.

"Yes, yes!" muttered Barrymaine, passing a hand across his brow. "Listen, then! Chichester knows, he knows, I tell you! He came to me, three days ago, and questioned me, and s-so I—I told him everything—everything!

"But I had to, Beverley, I had to, and then he laughed, and I t-tried to k-kill him, but he got away and left me alone with—*him*. He's always near me now—always c-close behind me where I can't quite s-see him, only sometimes I hear him ch-choke . . . oh, my God, Beverley, choke as he did—that night!

"I r-ran away to escape him, but—oh, Beverley—he's followed me, he was here a moment ago—I heard him, I t-tell you! Oh, Beverley, don't l-look as if you think me m-mad, I'm not! I know it's all an illusion, of c-course, but . . ."

"Yes," said Barnabas gently; "but what of Cleone?"

"Cleone? Oh, God help me, Beverley, she's going to g-give herself to that devil—to buy his silence!"

"What!" exclaimed Barnabas. "What do you mean?"

"I got this today—read and see!" said Barrymaine, and drew from his bosom-pocket a crumpled letter.

Barnabas took it and, smoothing it out, read these words:

> *Ronald dear, I'm sorry I didn't let you kiss me good-bye. So sorry that I am going to do all that a woman can to save you. Mr. Chichester has learned your awful secret, and I am the price of his silence.*
>
> *So, because of my promise to our dying mother, and because life can hold nothing for me now, because life and death are alike to me now, I am going to marry him tonight, at his house at Headcorn.*
>
> *Good-bye, Ronald dear, and that God may forgive and save you in this life and hereafter is the undying prayer of*
> *Your sister,*
> *Cleone*

Barnabas refolded the letter, gave it back to Barrymaine, and took out his watch.

"It is a long way to Headcorn," he said. "I must start at once!"

Committing Barrymaine to the care of Peterby, Barnabas took his coat and set off for the stables where his horse was kept.

Chapter Nine

Over Westminster Bridge galloped Barnabas, on through the roaring din of traffic.

On sped the great black horse, his pace increasing as the traffic lessened, on and on along the old Kent road, up the hill at New Cross and down again, and so through Lewisham to the open country beyond.

Presently, out of the dimness ahead, lights twinkled, growing ever brighter, and the town of Bromley was before him.

Then he was out upon the open road again where hedge and barn and tree seemed to leap at him from the dark, only to vanish in the dimness beyond.

On and on galloped the great black horse, until at last Barnabas reached the village of Headcorn and then on to the gates of a large house that he knew to be Ashleydown.

And at the very moment that his horse

reached the gates, Barnabas beheld the twinkling lights of an approaching chaise.

"Stop!" cried Barnabas.

Uttering a frightened oath, the postillion pulled up with a jerk, but as the chaise came to a standstill a window rattled down. Then Barnabas lowered his pistol, and coming up beside the chaise looked down into the troubled face of the Lady Cleone.

Her cheeks were very pale in the light of the lanterns and upon her dark lashes was the glitter of tears.

"You! Is it you . . . Barnabas?" she whispered. "I . . . I've been hoping you would come!"

"Then you expected me? You knew I should come?"

"Yes, Barnabas. I . . . I hoped you would see my letter to Ronald . . . that was why I wrote it! And I prayed that you might come. . . ."

"Why?"

"Because I . . . oh, Barnabas, I'm afraid!"

"You were going to Chichester?"

"Yes, Barnabas."

"You don't—love him, do you?"

"Love him! Oh, God!"

Barnabas saw her shudder violently.

"Yet you were going to him."

"To save my brother. But now . . . God help me, I can't do it! Oh, it's too hateful, and . . . and I am afraid, Barnabas.

"I ought to have been at Ashleydown an hour ago, but oh, I . . . I couldn't, it was too horrible . . . I couldn't! So I came the longest way. I made the post-boy drive very slowly; I . . . I was

220

waiting for . . . you, Barnabas, praying that you would come to me. . . ."

"Because you were afraid, My Lady?"

"Yes, Barnabas.".

"And behold, I am here!" said Barnabas.

But now, seeing the quiver of her white hands, and the light in her eyes, a sudden glow that was not of the lanterns, he turned his head and resolutely looked away.

"I am here, My Lady, to take you back home again," he said.

"Home? Ah, no, no . . . I have no home now! Oh, Barnabas," she whispered, "take me, take me away . . . to my brother. Let us go away from England tonight . . . anywhere. Only take me with you, Barnabas!"

"My Lady, why do you tempt me? I am only an Amateur Gentleman; why do you tempt me so?"

As he spoke, he wheeled his horse and motioned to the flinching post-boy.

"Turn!" he commanded.

But now the chaise-door was flung open and Cleone sprang down to the road.

"Let me pass!"

"To Chichester?"

"Yes, God help me. Since you force me to it! Let me go!"

"Get back into the chaise, My Lady."

"No," she answered; and though her face was hidden now, he knew that she was weeping.

"I'm going on now to Ashleydown, to save Ronald, to redeem the promise I gave to our mother. I must, I must . . . and oh, nothing matters to me any more, so let me go!"

Barnabas sighed, slipped the pistol into his pocket, and dismounted, but, being upon his feet, he staggered; then, before even she knew, he had caught her in his arms.

In that moment he looked down, and so stood there, bound by the spell of her beauty, forgetful of all else in the world, for the light of the lanterns was all about them, and Cleone's eyes were looking up into his.

"Barnabas, don't let me go . . . save me from . . . that!"

"Ah, Cleone, oh, My Lady, do you doubt me still? Can you think that I should fail you? Oh, my dear, I've found a way, and mine is a better way than yours. Be comforted, then, and trust me, Cleone."

Then she stirred in his embrace, and, sighing, hid her face close against him, and with her face hidden she said:

"Yes, yes . . . I do trust you, Barnabas, utterly, utterly! Take me away with you . . . tonight . . . take me to Ronald. Let us go away together, no matter where, so long as we go together, Barnabas."

Now when she said this, she could feel how his arms tightened about her, could hear how his breath caught, sudden and sharp, and although she kept her face hidden from him, well she knew what look was in his eyes; therefore, she lay trembling a little, sighing a little, and with fast-beating heart.

In a while Barnabas spoke:

"My Lady, would you trust yourself to a Publican's son?"

"If he would not be too proud to take me, Barnabas."

"Oh, My Lady, can't you see that if I—if I take you with me tonight, you must be with me always?"

Cleone sighed.

"And I am a discredited impostor, the—the jest of every Club in London. But you, you were born for higher and greater fortune than to become the wife of a humble farming fellow, and consequently . . ."

"But I can make excellent butter, Barnabas," she paused, and sighed, stealing a glance up to him, "and I can cook a little."

And seeing the sudden witchery of her swift-drooping lashes, Barnabas forgot his stern resolutions and stooped his head so that he might kiss the glory of her hair.

But in that moment she turned, swiftly and suddenly, and yielded him her lips, soft and warm and passionate with youth and all the joy of life.

And, borne away upon that kiss, it seemed to Barnabas, for one brief mad-sweet instant, that all things might be possible; if they started now they might reach London in the dawn, and, staying only for Barrymaine, be aboard ship by evening!

And it was a wide world, a very fair world, and with this woman beside him . . .

"It would be so—so very easy!" he said slowly.

"Yes, it will be very easy!" she whispered.

"Too easy!" he said, beginning to frown.

"You are so helpless and lonely, and I want you so bitterly, Cleone! Yes, it would be very easy. But you taught me once that a man must ever choose the harder way, and this is the harder way—to love you, to long for you, and to bid you good-bye!"

"Oh, Barnabas!"

"You are safe now," he said. "As for Ronald, if Chichester's silence can save him, you need grieve no more, and . . ."

"Ah! What do you mean?"

"That I must go, My Lady; and oh, my dear love, this harder way is very hard to tread. If we should meet no more after tonight, remember that I loved you—as I always have done and always must, humble fellow though I am.

"Yes, I think I love you as well as any fine gentleman of them all, and—Cleone—good-bye!"

"Barnabas!" she cried. "Tell me what you mean to do. . . . Oh, Barnabas, where are you going?"

And now she reached out her hands as though to stay him. But even so he drew away, and, wheeling his horse, pointed towards the twinkling lights.

"Drive on!" he cried to the post-boy.

"Barnabas, wait!"

But as Cleone strove desperately to open the door, the chaise lurched forward, and the horses broke into a gallop. And Barnabas, sitting there beneath the ancient finger-post, saw imploring hands stretched out towards him, heard a desolate cry, and then he was alone.

* * *

A distant clock was striking the hour as Barnabas rode in through the rusted gates of Ashleydown, tethered his horse, and walked towards the house.

Now, as he went, he took out one of his pistols, cocked it, and, with it ready in his hand, went to the window and peered into the room.

It was a long, low chamber with a fireplace at one end, and there, his frowning gaze upon the blazing logs, sat Mr. Chichester.

Then Barnabas raised the pistol-butt, beat in the window, loosened the catch, and, as Mr. Chichester sprang to his feet, opened the casement and stepped into the room.

For a long moment neither spoke, while eyes met and questioned eyes, those of Barnabas wide and bright, Mr. Chichester's narrowed to shining slits.

Indeed, as they fronted each other thus, each was the opposite of the other: Barnabas leaning in the window, his pistol-hand hidden behind him, a weary, bedraggled figure mired from heel to head; Mr. Chichester standing rigidly erect, immaculate of dress from polished boot to snowy cravat.

"Sir," said Barnabas, "give me leave to tell you that the Lady Cleone will not keep her appointment here tonight."

"Ahh!" said Mr. Chichester slowly, and, staring at Barnabas under his drawn brows, added, "you mean. . . ?"

"That she was safely at home three-quarters of an hour ago."

Mr. Chichester's eyes once more narrowed to
225

shining slits, with the scar burning redly upon his cheek.

"So you have dared to interfere again? You have dared to come here to tell me so?"

"No, Sir," answered Barnabas, shaking his head, "I have come here to kill you!"

Barnabas spoke very gently, but as Mr. Chichester beheld his calm eyes and his grimly smiling mouth, his own eyes widened suddenly, his clenched fingers opened, and he reached out towards the bell-rope.

"Stop!" said Barnabas, and, speaking, levelled his pistol.

"Ah!" Mr. Chichester sighed, falling back a step. "You mean to murder me, do you?"

"I said 'kill,' though yours is the better word, perhaps. Here are two pistols, you will observe; one is for you and one for me. But first I must trouble you to lock the door yonder and bring me the key. Lock it, I say!"

Very slowly, and with his eyes fixed in a wide stare upon the threatening muzzle of the weapon Barnabas held, Mr. Chichester crossed to the door, hesitated, turned the key, drew it from the lock, stood with it balanced in his hand for a moment, and then tossed it towards Barnabas.

"Now, Sir, take up your pistol."

"No!"

"Then," said Barnabas, "as God is above, I'll shoot you where you stand—but first I'll count three!"

Once more he levelled the pistol he held.

Mr. Chichester sighed a fluttering sigh, and

with his burning gaze upon Barnabas he stepped forward and laid his hand upon the chair-back, but in the act of sitting down he paused.

"The candles—a little more light—the candles," he muttered; and turning, he crossed to the hearth and raised his hand to a branched silver candlestick that stood upon the mantel.

But in the moment that his left hand closed upon this, his right hand darted upon another object that lay there, and, quick as a flash, he spun round and fired point-blank.

While the report yet rang on the air, Barnabas staggered, swayed, and, uttering a gasp, sank down weakly into the chair.

But as Mr. Chichester watched him, his eyes wide, his lips parted, and the pistol yet smoking in his hand, Barnabas leaned forward, and, steadying his elbow on the table, very, very slowly raised and levelled his weapon.

And now, as he fronted that deadly barrel, Mr. Chichester's face grew suddenly livid and haggard, while upon his brow the sweat had started and was rolling down his cheeks.

Then, all at once, upon this silence broke another sound, the grind of wheels and the hoof-strokes of madly galloping horses.

Mr. Chichester uttered a gasping cry and pointed toward the window.

"Cleone," he whispered. "It's Cleone! She's coming! In God's name—wait!"

The galloping hoofs drew rapidly nearer, stopped suddenly, and as Barnabas, hesitating, glanced towards the window, it was flung wide and somebody came leaping through—a wild, terrible figure; and as he turned in the light of the candles, Barnabas looked into the distorted face of Ronald Barrymaine.

For a moment he stood, his glowing eyes staring at Mr. Chichester, and as he stood thus, fixing Mr. Chichester with that awful, unwavering stare, a smile twisted his pallid lips, and he said very softly:

"The luck's with me at l-last—we're in time, I've g-got him! Come in, D-Dig, and bring the tools. I—I've g-got him!"

Hereupon Mr. Smivvle stepped into the room; haggard of eye he looked, and beneath his arm he carried a familiar oblong box.

At the sight of Barnabas he started, and, crossing the room hastily, he set the box upon the table and caught him by the arm.

"Stop him, Beverley—stop him!" he whispered hurriedly. "Barry's gone mad, I think—insisted on coming here. Devil of a time getting away; Bow Street Runners—hard behind us now."

Barrymaine crossed to the hearth and stood there warming his hands at the blaze, but even so, he turned his head so that he could keep his eyes always directed at Chichester's pale face.

"I'm w-warming my pistol-hand, mustn't be cold or s-stiff tonight, you see. Oh, I tell you the luck's with me at last! He's dragged me down to hell, but tonight I'm g-going to take him with me."

Even as Barrymaine spoke, warming himself at the fire, he kept his burning gaze upon Mr.

Chichester's pale face, while Barnabas leaned and twisted in his chair, and Mr. Smivvle busied himself with the oblong box.

With shaking hands Mr. Smivvle took out the duelling-pistols, one by one, and laid them on the table.

Mr. Chichester then took up one of the weapons.

"Ah—he's chosen, I s-see. Now we'll t-take opposite corners of the room and f-fire when you give the word, eh?"

As Barrymaine spoke, he advanced to the table and took up the remaining pistol. Then, with it cocked in his hand, he backed away to the corner beside the hearth.

Mr. Chichester strode to the opposite corner of the long room, and, turning, stood there with folded arms.

"Sirs," said he, "I shall most certainly kill him, and I call upon you to witness that it was forced upon me."

Now as his voice died away, through the open window came a faint sound that might have been the drumming of horse-hoofs, soft and faint in the distance.

"Gentlemen," said Mr. Smivvle, with shaking hands steadying himself against the panelling, "The word will be—'Ready!' One! . . . Two! . . . Three!—Fire! Do you understand?"

An eager "Yes" from Barrymaine, a slight nod from Chichester.

"S-speak! Will you s-speak, Dig?"

"Oh, Barry—my dear boy, yes! Ready?"

229

At the word, the two pistols were raised and levelled, almost on the instant, and with his haggard eyes turned towards Barrymaine's corner, Mr. Smivvle spoke again:

"One! . . . Two! . . . Three!"

A flash, a single, deafening report, and Ronald Barrymaine lurched sideways, caught at the wall, swayed backwards into the corner, and leaned there.

"Coward—you fired too soon!" cried Smivvle, turning upon Mr. Chichester in sudden frenzy. "Villain! Rogue! You fired too soon.

"Oh, Barry—you're bleeding! By God, he's hit you!"

"Of c-course, Dig—he never m-misses— neither do I! W-watch now—ah!—hold me up, Dig—so! Now, stand away!"

But even as Barrymaine, livid of brow and with teeth hard-clenched, steadied himself for the shot, loud and clear upon the night came the thudding of swift-galloping horse-hoofs.

And now for the first time Barrymaine's gaze left Chichester's face, and fixed itself upon the open casement instead.

"Ha!" he cried. "Here comes the Constable at last, D-Dig, and with his hangman at his elbow! But he's t-too late, Dig, he's too l-late; I'm going, but I mean to take our friend—our d-dear friend Chichester—w-with me! Look now!"

As he spoke he raised his arm, and there came the stunning report of the pistol and a puff of blinding smoke; but when it cleared, Mr. Chichester still stood up rigidly in his corner, but as he stood, he lifted his hand suddenly to his mouth,

230

glanced at his fingers, and then stared at them with wide, horrified eyes.

Then his pistol clattered to the floor and he coughed, a hideous strangling sound. Coughing still, he took a swift pace forward, striving to speak, but sank to his knees.

Even then he strove desperately to utter something, but with it still unspoken he sank down upon his hands, and thence slowly upon his face, and lay there, very still and quiet.

Then Barrymaine laughed, an awful, gasping laugh, and began to edge himself along the wall. Having come to that inanimate figure, he stood awhile, watching it with gloating eyes.

Presently he said in a harsh whisper:

"He's dead—quite dead, you see! And he was my f-friend, which was bad! And I trusted him—which was w-worse. A rogue always, Dig, and a l-liar!"

Then Barrymaine groaned, and groaned again, spurred that quiet form weakly with his foot, and so pitched down headlong across it.

Now as they lay thus, they together made a great cross upon the floor.

But presently shadows moved beyond the open window, and a voice said:

"In the King's name! I arrest Ronald Barrymaine for the murder of Jasper Gaunt—in the King's name, gentlemen!"

But now, very slow and painfully, Ronald Barrymaine raised himself upon his hands, lifted his heavy head, and spoke in a feeble voice:

"Oh, M-Master Hangman, y-you're too l-late —j-just too late!"

And so, like a weary child setting himself to rest, he pillowed his head upon his arm, and, sighing—fell asleep.

Then the man stepped forward very softly, and beholding that placid young face with its tender, smiling lips, and the lashes that drooped so dark against the deep pallor of the cheek, he took off his broad-brimmed hat and stood there with bent head.

But another figure had followed him, and now sprang towards Barnabas with supporting arms outstretched, and in that moment Barnabas sighed, and, falling forward, lay there sprawled across the table, with John Peterby's agonised face bent over him.

*   *   *

The sunlight was flooding in at the open lattice. And by this Barnabas, opening drowsy eyes and hearkening with drowsy ears, judged it was yet early morning.

He lay very still and full of a great content because of the glory of the sun and the merry piping of the birds. But, little by little he became aware that he lay in a bed, undressed, and that his arm and shoulder were bandaged.

With great caution he lifted his free hand to his neck and began to feel for a certain ribbon that should be there.

And presently, having found the ribbon, his questing fingers followed it down to his bosom until they touched a little, clumsily wrought linen bag that he had fashioned, once upon a time, and in which he had been wont to carry the dried-up wisp of what had once been a fragrant, scarlet rose.

"Why, Barnabas!" said the Duchess, very gently. "Dear boy . . . what is it? Ah! You've found it then, already . . . your sachet? There . . . let me open it for you . . . so! Now, while I hold it, see what is inside."

Then, wondering, Barnabas slipped a clumsy thumb and finger into the little bag, and behold, the faded wisp had become transfigured and bloomed again in all its virgin freshness!

For in his hand there lay a great scarlet rose, as sweet and fresh and fragrant as though for all the world it had been plucked that very morning.

"But," murmured the drowsy Barnabas, speaking with an effort, "it—was—dead—long—ago. . . ?"

"Yet behold, it is alive again!" said the Duchess.

"And oh, Barnabas dear, if a withered, faded wisp may bloom again . . . so may a woman's faith and love. There, there, dear boy! Close your eyes and go to sleep again."

So, being very weary, Barnabas closed his eyes, and, with the touch of her small, cool fingers in his hair, fell fast asleep.

Now as Barnabas lay thus, lost in slumber, he dreamt a dream.

It seemed to him that he was lying out amidst the green, dewy freshness of Annersley Wood. And, as he lay there, grievously hurt, lo, there came to him one hasting, light-footed, through the green, one for whom he seemed to have been waiting long and patiently, one as sweet and fresh and fair as the golden morning, and as tender as the Spirit of Womanhood.

She leaned above him and her hands touched him, hands very soft and cool, and gentle, upon his brow, upon his cheek; and every touch was a caress.

Slowly, slowly her arms came about him in a warm, clinging embrace, arms strong and protecting, which drew his weary head to the swell of a bosom and pillowed it sweetly there.

And, clasping him thus, she sighed over him and wept, though very silently, and stooped her lips to him to kiss his brow, his slumbrous eyes, and, last of all, his mouth.

So, because of this dream, Barnabas lay in deep and utter content, for it seemed that Happiness had come to him after all, and of its own accord.

But in a while he stirred and sighed, and presently opened dreamy eyes, and thus it chanced that he beheld the door of his chamber, and the door was quivering as though it had but just closed.

Then, as he lay watching it, sleepy-eyed, it opened again slow and noiselessly.

John Peterby entered softly, took a step towards the bed, but, seeing that Barnabas was awake, he stopped and so stood there very still.

Suddenly Barnabas smiled and reached out a hand to him.

"Why John," said he, "my faithful John—is it you?"

"Sir," murmured Peterby, and coming forward took that extended hand, looking down at Barnabas joyful-eyed, and would have spoken, yet uttered no other word.

"John," said Barnabas, glancing round the faded splendours of the bed-chamber, "where am I, pray?"

"At Ashleydown, sir."

"Ashleydown!" repeated Barnabas, wrinkling his brow.

"Sir, you have been very ill."

"Ah, yes, I was shot, I remember—last night, I think?"

"Sir, it happened over three weeks ago."

"Three weeks!" repeated Barnabas, sitting up with an effort. "Three weeks, John? Oh, impossible!"

"You have been very near death, Sir. Indeed, I think you would have died but for the tender nursing and unceasing care of . . ."

"Ah, God, bless her! Where is she, John—where is the Duchess?"

"Her Grace went out driving this morning, Sir."

"This morning? Why, I was talking with her this morning—only a little while ago."

"That was yesterday morning, Sir."

"Oh!" said Barnabas, hand to head. "Do you mean that I have slept the clock round?"

"Yes, Sir."

"Hum!" said Barnabas. "Consequently, I'm hungry, John, deuced sharp set—ravenous, John!"

"That, Sir," quoth Peterby, smiling his rare

smile, "that is the best news I've heard this three weeks and more, and your chicken-broth is ready. . . ."

"Chicken-broth!" exclaimed Barnabas. "For shame, John. Bring me a steak, do you hear?"

"But, Sir," Peterby remonstrated, shaking his head, yet with his face brightening, "indeed, I . . ."

"Or a chop, John, or ham and eggs—I'm hungry, I tell you."

"Excellent!" Peterby laughed, nodding his head. "But the Doctor, Sir . . ."

"Doctor!" cried Barnabas with a snort. "What do I want with Doctors? I'm well, John. Bring me my clothes."

"Clothes, Sir!" exclaimed Peterby, aghast. "Impossible, Sir! No, no!"

"Yes, yes, John—I'm going to get up."

"But, Sir . . ."

"This very moment! My clothes, John, my clothes!"

"Indeed, Sir, I . . ."

"John Peterby," said Barnabas, scowling blackly, "you will oblige me with my garments this instant—obey me, Sir!"

But hereupon, while Barnabas scowled and Peterby hesitated, puckered of brow yet joyful of eye, there came the sound of wheels on the drive below and the slam of a coach-door, whereat Peterby crossed to the window and, glancing out, heaved a sigh of relief.

"Who is it?" demanded Barnabas, his scowl blacker than ever.

"Her Grace has returned, Sir."

"Very good, John! Present my compliments

and say I will wait upon her as soon as I'm dressed."

But hardly had Peterby left the room with this message than the door opened again and Her Grace of Camberhurst appeared, who catching sight of Barnabas sitting up shock-headed among his pillows, uttered a little glad cry and hurried to him.

"Why, Barnabas!" she exclaimed, "oh, Barnabas!"

With the words she stooped, quick and sudden, yet in the most matter-of-fact manner in the world, and kissed him lightly on the brow.

"Oh, dear me!" she cried, beginning to pat and smooth his tumbled pillows, "how glad I am to see you able to frown again, though indeed you look dreadfully ferocious Barnabas!"

"I'm very hungry, Duchess!"

"Of course you are, Barnabas, and God bless you for it!"

"A steak, Madam, or a chop, I think...."

"Would be excellent, Barnabas!"

"And I wish to get up, Duchess."

"To be sure you do, Barnabas, there, lie down, so!"

"But, Madam, I am firmly resolved—I'm quite determined to get up, at once...."

"Quite so, dear Barnabas, lay your head back on the pillow! Dear me, how comfortable you look! And now, you are hungry, you say?

"Then I'll sit here and gossip to you while you take your chicken-broth! You may bring it in, Mr. Peterby."

"Chicken-broth!" snarled Barnabas, frown-

237

ing blacker than ever. "But, Madam, I tell you I won't have the stuff. I repeat, Madam, that I am quite determined to . . ."

"There, there, rest your poor tired head, so! And it's all a delicious jelly when it's cold, I mean the chicken-broth, of course, not your head. Ah! You may give it to me, Mr. Peterby, and the spoon . . . thank you! Now, Barnabas!"

And hereupon, observing the firm set of Her Grace's mouth, and the authoritative flourish of the spoon she held in her small though imperious hand, Barnabas submitted.

Lying back among his pillows in sulky dignity, he swallowed the decoction in sulky silence, and thereafter lay hearkening sulkily to her merry chatter until he had sulked himself to sleep again.

* * *

His third awakening was much like the first in that the room was full of sunshine and the air vibrant with the song of birds.

This time, seeing that there was no one in the room with him, he got out of bed and struggled to put on his clothes.

"Gracious heavens, he's actually up, and dressed! Oh, Lud, Barnabas, what does this mean?"

Barnabas started and turned to find the Duchess regarding him from the doorway.

"It means that, thanks to you, Duchess, I am well again and . . ."

"And as pale as a goblin . . . no, I mean a ghost. Lud, Barnabas . . . how thin you are!"

"But strong enough to go on my way. . . ."

"Way? What way? Which way?"

"Home, Duchess."

"Home, home indeed? You are home, this is your home. Ashleydown is yours now."

"Yes," Barnabas nodded, "I suppose it is, but I shall never live here, I leave today. I am going back to my father and Natty Bell."

"And to that Inn?"

"Yes, for a time, but . . ."

"Ha . . . a Publican!"

"There is a farm nearby, I shall probably . . ."

"Ha . . . a farmer!"

"Raise horses, Madam."

"Horses!" cried the Duchess, and sniffed again. "What of your dreams? What of London? What of Society?"

"They were only dreams," answered Barnabas; "in place of them I shall have my father."

"Secondly, Sir, what of your fine ambitions?"

"It will be my ambition, henceforth, to breed good horses, Madam."

"What of Cleone?"

"Cleone! Ah yes—Cleone!"

"You love her, I suppose?"

"So much—so very much that she shall never marry an Inn-keeper's son, or a discredited . . ."

"Don't be so hatefully proud, Barnabas. Oh, dear me, what a superbly virtuous, heroic fool you are, Barnabas! When you met her at the cross-roads, for instance . . . oh, why didn't you . . . run off with her and marry her, as any ordinary human man would have done?"

She threw out her hands and exclaimed:

"Dear heaven, it would have been so deliciously romantic! And such an easy way out of it!"

"Yes, so easy that it was wrong!"

"Bah!" cried the Duchess very fiercely as she rose and turned to the door. "I've no patience with you! I planned for you to be married from my house in Berkeley Square and for all my friends—my real friends—to be there."

"Ah, Duchess," Barnabas said, staying her with pleading hands, "can't you see—don't you understand? Were she, this proud lady, my wife, I would be haunted, day and night, by the fear that someday, sooner or later, she would find me to be—not of her world—not the man she would have me, but only a Publican's son, after all. Now you see why I dare not?"

"Oh, Pride! Pride! Do you expect her to come to you then; would you have her go down on her knees to you and beg you to marry her?"

Barnabas turned to the window again and stood there awhile, staring blindly out beyond the swaying green of trees.

When at last he spoke his voice was hoarse and there was a bitter smile upon his lips.

"Yes, Duchess, before such great happiness could be mine she must come to me, she must go down upon her knees—proud lady that she is —and beg this Inn-keeper's son to marry her. So you see, Duchess, I shall never marry!"

Now when at last Barnabas looked round, the Duchess had her back to him, nor did she turn even when she spoke.

"Then you are going back to your father?"

"Yes, Madam."

"Today?"

"Yes, Madam."

"Then ... good-bye, Barnabas!"

And thus, without even glancing at him, the Duchess went out of the room and closed the door softly behind her.

*   *   *

That evening, Barnabas Beverley, the Amateur Gentleman, found himself back at the old Greyhound Inn, plain Barnabas Barty again, welcomed by his father and Natty Bell. After dinner they sat talking by the fire.

"And now, Barnabas," said John slowly, " 'ow might your shoulder be now?"

"Nearly well, Father."

"Good," John nodded, "very good! I thought as you was going to die, Barnabas, lad. They all did—even the Duchess and the Lady . . . and the Doctors, Barnabas."

"Were you going to say—Lady Cleone, Father? Have you ever seen her, then?"

But at this moment the door opened and two neat, mob-capped maids entered and began to spread a cloth upon the table. Scarcely had they departed when in came Natty Bell.

"Oh, Natty Bell!" exclaimed John, beckoning him nearer, "Come to this lad of ours—do, he's axing me questions, one atop of t'other till I don't know what! 'Do I know Lady Cleone?' says he, next it'll be 'how' and 'what' and 'where'—tell him all about it, Natty, do."

241

"Why then, Barnabas, when you were so ill, d' ye see, John and me used to drive over frequent to see how you was. But you being so ill, we weren't allowed to go up and see you so she used to come down to us and talk of you. Ah! And very sweet and gentle she was.

"But one day, Barnabas, after we'd called a good many times, she *did* take us up to see you— didn't she, John? And you was a-lying there with shut eyes and being out o' your mind, and not seeing us—delirious, d' ye see, Barnabas, you began to speak.

" 'No,' says you very fierce, 'No! I love you so much that I can never ask you to be the wife of Barnabas Barty. Mine must be the harder way, always. The harder way! The harder way!'

"And so we left you, but your voice follered us down the stairs—ah, and out o' the house, 'the harder way!' says you, 'the harder way'—over and over again. So now, Barnabas, we'd like the liberty to ax you, John and me, what you meant by it."

"It means that I have been all the way to London to learn what you, being so much wiser than I, tried to teach me—that a sow's ear is not a silk purse, nor ever can be," Barnabas replied. "Today, since I never can be a gentleman, I have come home so that you may teach me to be a man. And believe me, I have no regrets, none— none at all!"

He spoke fiercely, as if he expected them to argue, then went on:

"I mean to be very busy, to—to devote my

money to making us all happy. I have several ideas already, my head is full of schemes."

He smiled a little grimly and continued:

"For one thing, I'm going to carry out the improvements you suggested years ago for the dear old Hound, Father—and you and I, Natty, might buy the farm next door; it's for sale, I know, and go in for raising horses. Come, what do you say?"

"Well," answered Natty Bell, "I think, Barnabas, since you ax me so pointed-like, that you'd do much better in taking a wife and raising children."

"Ah—why not, lad?" His father nodded. "It be high time as you was thinking o' settling down, so why not get married and ha' done with it?"

"Because," answered Barnabas, frowning at the fire, "I can love only one woman in this world, and she is altogether beyond my reach, and—never can be mine—never."

"Ha!" said Natty Bell, getting up and staring down into the fire. "Remember this, Barnabas, when a woman sets her mind on anything, I've noticed as she generally manages to get it, one way or t'other. So I wouldn't be too sure if I was you."

Saying which, he nodded to John, above his son's drooping head, winked, and went silently out of the room.

Left alone with his son, John Barty sat awhile, and finally spoke:

"Barnabas, your—your—mother, God bless her sweet soul, was a great lady, but I married

243

her, and I don't think as she ever regretted it, lad.
Ye see, Barnabas, when a good woman really
loves a man, that man is the only man in the
world to her, and nothing else matters to her, because her love, being a good love, d' ye see—
makes him—almost worthy.

"The love of a good woman is a sweet thing,
lad, a wondrous thing, and may lift a man above
all cares and sorrows and may draw him up—ah!
—as high as heaven at last, and—well—there
y' are, Barnabas, dear lad."

Having said this, John Barty laid his great
hand lightly upon his son's bent head and followed
Natty Bell out of the room.

Soon, being full of despondent thoughts,
Barnabas looked and found himself alone amidst
the gathering shadows.

Straightaway he felt aggrieved, and wondered
why his father and Natty Bell should go off and
leave him in the dark hour just when he most
needed them.

He would have risen to seek them out, but,
in the act of doing so, caught one of his spurs in
the rug, and strove vainly to release himself, for
try how he would he might not reach down so far
because of the pain of his wounded shoulder.

And now, all at once, perhaps because he
found himself so helpless, or because of his loneliness and bodily weakness, the sudden tears
started to his eyes, hot and scalding, and cover-
ing his face, he groaned.

But in that moment of his need there came
one, borne on flying feet, to kneel beside him in
the fire-glow, and with swift, dexterous fingers to

do for him that which he could not do for himself.

But when it was done and he was free, she still knelt there with head bent, and her face hidden beneath the frill of her mob-cap.

"Thank—you!" he said very humbly. "I fear I am very awkward, but my shoulder is a little stiff."

But this strange serving-maid never moved, or spoke. And now, looking down at her shapely drooping figure, Barnabas began to tremble, all at once, and his fingers clenched themselves upon his chair-arms.

"Speak!" he whispered hoarsely.

Then the great mob-cap was shaken off, yet the face of this maid was still hid from him by reason of her hair that, escaping its fastenings, fell down, over bowed neck and white shoulders, rippling to the floor, a golden glory.

And now, beholding the shining splendour of this hair, his breath caught, and as one entranced, he gazed down at her, fearing to move.

"Cleone!" he said, breathily, at last.

So Cleone raised her head and looked at him, sighing a little, blushing a little, trembling a little, with eyes shy yet unashamed, the eyes of a maid.

"Oh, Barnabas," she murmured, "I am here on my knees. You wanted me on my knees, didn't you, Barnabas? So I am here to ask you . . ."

But now her dark lashes fluttered and fell, hiding her eyes from him.

"To beg you to marry me. Because I love you, Barnabas, and because, whatever else you may be, I know you are a man. So . . . if you really . . . want me, dear Barnabas, why . . . take me, because I am just . . . your woman."

"Want you!" he repeated. "Want you—oh, my Cleone!"

With a broken, inarticulate cry, he leaned down, and would have caught her fiercely against his heart, but she, ever mindful of his wound, stayed him with gentle hand.

"Oh, my dear . . . your shoulder!" she whispered.

So, clasping tender arms about him, she drew his weary head to her bosom and, holding him thus, covered him with the silken curtain of her hair, and in this sweet shade stooped and kissed him, his brow, his tearful eyes, and last of all, his mouth.

"Oh, Barnabas," she murmured, "was there ever, I wonder, a man so foolish and so very dear as you, or a woman quite so proud and happy as I?"

"Proud?" he answered. "But you are a great lady, and I am only . . ."

"My dear, dear man." Cleone sighed, clasping him a little more closely. "So; when will you marry me? For, oh, my Barnabas, if you must always choose to go the harder way . . . you must let me tread it with you, to the very end, my dear, brave, honourable man."

In a while, he looked down at Cleone where she knelt in his embrace, beholding all the charm and witchery of her, the high, proud carriage of her head, the grace and beauty of her shapely body, soft and warm with life and youth and love.

Barnabas sighed for very happiness.

Whereupon, she, glancing up and meeting this look, must needs droop her lashes at him, and blush, and tremble, all in a moment.

"But you are mine!" said Barnabas, answering the blush. "Mine, at last, forever and always."

"Forever, and always, dear Barnabas."

"And yet," said he, his clasp tightening, "I am so unworthy it almost seems that it cannot possibly be true, almost as if it were a dream."

"Ah, no, Barnabas, surely the dream is over and we are awake at last to joy and the fullness of life. And life has given me my heart's desire, and for you, my brave, strong, honourable man ... the Future lies all before you."

"Yes," said Barnabas, looking deep into her radiant eyes, "for me there is the Future—and you."

ABOUT THE EDITOR

BARBARA CARTLAND, the world's most famous romantic novelist, who is also an historian, playwright, lecturer, political speaker and television personality, has now written over 200 books. She has also had many historical works published and has written four autobiographies as well as the biographies of her mother and that of her brother Ronald Cartland, who was the first Member of Parliament to be killed in the last war. This book has a preface by Sir Winston Churchill. Barbara Cartland has sold 80 million books over the world, more than half of these in the U.S.A. She broke the world record in 1975 by writing twenty books in a year, and her own record in 1976 with twenty-one. In private life, Barbara' Cartland, who is a Dame of the Order of St. John of Jerusalem, has fought for better conditions and salaries for Midwives and Nurses. As President of the Royal College of Midwives (Hertfordshire Branch), she has been invested with the first Badge of Office ever given in Great Britain, which was subscribed to by the Midwives themselves. She has also championed the cause for old people and founded the first Romany Gypsy Camp in the world. Barbara Cartland is deeply interested in Vitamin Therapy and is President of the British National Association for Health.